A Brilliant Novel in the Works

M P Publishing Limited
6 Petaluma Boulevard North
Suite B6
Petaluma, CA 94952

Zalkow, Yuvi.
    A brilliant novel in the works / by Yuvi Zalkow.
    p. cm.
    ISBN 978-1-84982-165-0
    1. Jews--Fiction. 2. Israel--Fiction. 3. Portland
(Or.)--Fiction. I. Title.

PS3626.A6275B75 2012   813'.6
                                      QBI12-600075

A Brilliant Novel in the Works

By Yuvi Zalkow

for snuffalo

Contents

BOOK 5: IN THE END

CHAPTER 32: YUMMY
THROAT CLEARING
CHAPTER 33: BAD DATES
WHAT TO DO WITH SHOSHANA?
CHAPTER 34: ETHNIC PLOT DEVICE
CHAPTER 35: PALOOKAVILLE PEE PEE PARTY
CHAPTER 36: TRAITORS
CHAPTER 37: END OF BUSINESS
CHAPTER 38: BROTHER, CAN YOU SPARE A PALINDROME?
CHAPTER 39: OUT TO DRY
MOUNT PISGAH
CHAPTER 40: FROM UP HIGH
CHAPTER 41: WHAT DO YOU SEE?
ODE TO FATHER
CHAPTER 42: PEEK SOUL
CHAPTER 43: SAVE ME, JULIA
CHAPTER 44: A BANISHED TYPO

Book 1
GENESIS

Chapter One
Pantslessness

When my wife comes into the room and sees me in my underwear, with my $30 Lamy pen in my fist, and standing on my desk, she isn't terribly impressed with me and my work habits.

My home office is the smallest room in the house, but it still feels like a lot to take in from ten feet up. I thought my angst would weaken at this altitude.

"Jesus, Yuvi," Julia finally says, "you're getting awfully desperate." My wife shakes her head in that way that she can shake it and then reaches up to smack me on the ass in that way she can smack it.

"Not only that," she says, "but your underwear is torn in the back. Why won't you throw them away? They've been with you three times as long as I have."

"Hush!" I say. "I'm trying to work."

My wife heads back to the kitchen.

She has never been supportive of my creative process.

She is also what my mom would call a real gentile.

When I look down at the room these are the first three things that I notice:

There is a book called *Best Short Stories of 1997,* which my father bought me at a used bookstore, on the floor beside my desk. He bought it as a gift for me upon announcing that he had prostate cancer. What kind of person gives an "I have cancer!" gift?

There is a photograph of my wife's younger brother. The one with ulcerative colitis. The one we call Shmendrik. The one who reads faster and holds a job worse than anyone I know. It's a picture of Shmendrik and his girlfriend's eight-year-old daughter. They're doing push-ups. Both their jeans are pulled down so that his hairy butt and her munchkin butt are showing. This photo is on my desk because I love it, and also because I don't quite know what to do with it. He gave us two copies.

And there is that blank piece of paper underneath my feet.

My words feel more profound when I'm standing on my desk. Everything I say seems confident and proper. I wonder how many things I could get done from up here: ask for a bank loan, submit a book proposal, pray to my dead parents, write a peace treaty for the Middle East, ask my wife to take off her clothes and dance the way she did that one time.

From the kitchen, my wife asks me if I want a sandwich. I say that I do, but I beg her not to use mayonnaise or bacon.

My wife claims that without those two ingredients a BLT is worth nothing. I ask her if she'd use the word *bupkis* instead of nothing. And when I don't hear a response from the kitchen, I threaten that she's too gentile for me.

She yells out, "*Kush meer in tuches*," which is Yiddish for "kiss my ass." In the five years that we've been married, she has somehow gotten better at Yiddish than me.

I explain to her that an LT isn't so far away from a BLT. It's two-thirds complete, I say.

This is when she comes back into the room. Her hair is gentile red and she has gentile freckles and she wrinkles her gentile forehead when she's annoyed with me. Or when she's worried about her brother's health. Big issues and little issues all do the same thing to her face.

"You're wrong," she tells me from down there where all the mortals live. "You've destroyed the whole beauty of it."

As if we're talking about the Mona Lisa and not some absurd Protestant excuse for a sandwich. Imagine calling something beautiful that has neither pastrami nor rye bread.

I let her make me a BLT so that she'll leave me alone.

My wife wasn't as excited as I was about these photographs of her brother's ass. When she saw them, she closed her eyes and shook her head as if to say, "I love him in spite of this." But I love him because of this.

I was the one who named her younger brother Shmendrik. Why else would a thirty-five-year-old man from Iowa have a name like that? In Yiddish, it means someone who is clueless. If I didn't care for him so much I would have never given him that name.

I come down from the desk even though it means confronting that blank piece of paper.

My editor is quick to remind me that I owe her a novel. By quick, I mean that she doesn't even say hello before telling me about my overdue contractual obligation. And she's quick to remind me that my contract only allows for one collection of fragile little stories and that I've already done that. Years ago. She is quick to tell me that the world is different now than it was before. As if terrorists had bombed the world's demand for fragile little stories.

Ever since I realized that I owe her a novel—a real novel, not a pretend novel, but a thing full of the meat and bones and feathers and foreskin that any good novel must possess—what I'm writing these days is *bupkis*.

I've decided that I'm willing to lose three fingers and six toes for something to appear on the page. I'd take four toes off one foot and two off the other. At least one foot would still have a majority of toes intact.

When I told my wife what my editor said, my wife made it sound simple. "So write a novel," she said. And when I told her that I can't write a novel, she said, "So to hell with your editor. Keep writing your fragile little stories and find another way to make money."

She's always trying to solve my problems. My people don't tend to solve problems that easily. We don't even want to solve problems that easily. My people suffer. We're professional sufferers.

"Give it a rest with you and your people," my wife keeps telling me. "You're no more Jewish than Soon-Yi."

#

I thank my wife for the BLT and close the door to my office. A minute later she slips a paper towel under the door and I notice that she sneakily wrote "Luv u" on it. Which is sweet—even with the incorrect spelling—except that it reminds me of the note I found in her pants pocket.

My wife's L's are so loopy that I tilt my head to see if it says something else in there.

I put the plate with the Protestant sandwich on my blank page. The bacon sticks arrogantly out of my sandwich. While my wife helps recovering alcoholics and listens to secrets that have been bottled up for twenty-seven years, I scratch my ass through torn underwear and whine.

I resent that my fragile stories no longer work. But I'm not sure whom to resent.

ORIGIN OF SPECIES

We buried my mother in a Jewish cemetery in Atlanta. As she was dying, she forgot how to speak English. It was Hebrew all the way down. She was from Israel. She met my father there, moved with him to Atlanta, and they raised me in the States. Matrilineally, my mother was the seventh generation born in Jerusalem. Her father lived and died in Jerusalem, but he was born in Iraq, in Basra, back when there was a Jewish community in that land.

I scattered my father's ashes in the Davidson River, in the Pisgah National Forest, in North Carolina, where he was born. He lived in many places, including Atlanta and Israel. His parents were born in Poland. They escaped Hitler, passed through Ellis Island, and lived out their days in this North Carolina forest.

I was born in the Negev desert in Israel. I grew up in Atlanta. And now I live in Portland, Oregon, where Israel feels further away than Uranus. I like to tell people that I'm lost between worlds, but I don't really know which worlds I'm between.

A year before he died, my father told me he wanted to be cremated. This isn't something typically done by Jews, especially after the Holocaust, but it was what he wanted. These mountains feel like my home, he said to me. We were standing by his favorite river and we listened to the water for some time before he spoke again. Maybe we're a lot like salmon, he said. At this point in his life, he was a fly fisherman more than anything else and he felt that everything could be better understood through fishing metaphors. I asked him what he meant about us being like salmon because I often didn't get his metaphors. Just like salmon, he told me, we want to come back to where we started. We want to make a mark on this earth. And once we make some kind of mark, we're ready to die.

Chapter Two
Masquerading

"Get your pants on," Julia tells me. "We're going out."

"I don't want to put my pants on," I say. "Why don't you take your pants off?"

She says, "If you want me to be pantsless at the Righteous Room in front of my brother and his girlfriend, then just say the word."

It's a game of chicken and she knows I can't win. I already get jealous of the men who stare at her when we go out in public.

"Okay," I say. "You win. Pants all around."

She's right that I need to put on my pants. She's right that I'm not as Jewish as I advertise. My wife is right that my writing is getting too desperate these days. She's right about a lot of things.

But I've got a pretty good list of things that she doesn't know. She doesn't know that I give her brother $300 a month for his debts. She doesn't know that I found a note on a cocktail napkin in her pants pocket that said in a mess of a man's handwriting, "Save me, Julia." Scribbled by one of those men who can no longer distinguish between capital and lowercase, cursive and print, married and single. She doesn't know that the dreams about my dad are getting so bad that I've been using her brother's painkillers to get some sleep. My wife doesn't know I've started making cuts on my ass with a razor blade (again) so that when I sit down, I feel the burn something awful. She doesn't know I've quit going to my most recent therapist. She doesn't know exactly how desperate I've become.

You should know: I'm not an asshole. I don't want to keep these things from her. It's just that one little thing became two little things, and then, five years later, we are living our lives within the secrets behind our lives. Even meaningless ones—I don't tell my wife that I hide pictures of her as a child under the mattress. In one picture, she's in pigtails and making a frowny face like someone stole her lollipop. I look at them every morning after she goes to work.

"You need to get out of the house more," my wife keeps telling me. "It's not good for you to be here all the time. Who knows what happens all those hours that I'm gone. Go to a café. Hang around other people. Maybe you'll meet another writer who's as scared to put on their pants as you are."

"Maybe," she continues, "if you got out of the house more, you'd stop brooding so much about your damn editor and get something done."

I will need to pay back the advance that I received—money I no longer have—if I don't deliver her a novel.

My editor also says that I can't keep whining about my therapists, like in my other stories, and I can't keep talking about masturbation and my childhood and my family. Enough about my father and his fishing already.

My novel can't be about me writing a novel.

For some reason, my editor also doesn't want to read another story about my recent bout of impotence or my desire to be spanked while tied up or my preferred method for using a razor to make cuts on my ass.

She warned me: my novel can't be a collection of essays masquerading as a novel.

When I didn't respond to her requirements, she said, "Yuvi, this isn't an unreasonable request. I know you can do this."

When I didn't respond to that, she said, "Yuvi, what are you so scared of?"

When I didn't respond to that, she said, "Hello? Yuvi? Are you there?"

And then she hung up.

BLACKING OUT

"Yuvi? Yuvi? Can you hear me? Are you there? Did it work?"

I could hear him, but I couldn't respond. I smiled. I know I was smiling, but my eyes were closed and would not open. Through my tube socks, I could feel the Lego pieces I was stepping on. Every corner of my room had wandering pieces that never made it back to the shoebox.

I was standing against the wall. I was standing in my bedroom. I mostly knew that this was the case. And Ezra's hands were pressed against my chest. I could feel the heat from his palm, though that heat seemed to come from some kind of fire inside of me.

There was also a part of me that wasn't in my bedroom, was floating with the clouds and looking down at our houses, free from everything I wanted to be free from. The clouds were fluffy and cartoony, the kind you can really lounge around on.

Ezra and I were about ten at the time, and he lived across the street from me. We played together every day after school—at his house, at my house, in the forest, wherever—until we each had to go home for dinner. That day, he had just learned this cool trick, one we had been trying on each other all afternoon.

Here were his instructions: Lean against the wall. Bend over with your head hanging upside down for at least three minutes. Stand up faster than hell and hold your breath while the other person presses both their hands as hard as they can against your chest. If things go well, then you go limp within twenty seconds.

"I promise I'll catch you if you fall over," Ezra said to me. And when I didn't respond, he said, "Trust me, you won't die. I'll even go first."

I was thinking that this was the coolest thing I'd ever heard anyone tell me. I loved how it went when people blacked out in the movies, the look in their eyes like they just came back from being a different person from a different world. I was thrilled with the idea of having that moment where I'm so lost that I need to say, "Where am I? Who am I?"

We fought over who would go first. He argued that it was his idea to do this in the first place, and I couldn't refute that. But I still couldn't get him to black out no matter how hard I pressed on his chest. And then he couldn't get me to black out. And then I tried it on him again. And so on, until my third time, when I hovered over those cartoony clouds in my semi-conscious trance.

When I came to, Ezra told me that I was in a trance for a full minute. He said I was smiling this goofy smile like I was dreaming about Nari Tanaka. Nari was the Japanese girl in my class that I was in love with that year—and for six more years—without ever doing a thing about it.

As a kid, I worried. There were always at least one or two horrible, embarrassing things that kept me up at night. At various times, these worries included: too much hair growing out of my armpits, too ticklish to ever have a girlfriend, a tumor in my brain/arm/leg/butt, a crooked penis, a crooked stream of piss, being Jewish around a bunch of beautiful suburban WASPs, an inability to kick a kickball, having skin the color of a Middle Eastern terrorist, and my dumb smile.

For one minute, this trance made my world of armpit hair, crooked penises, and dumb smiles completely disappear. I let myself slowly fall down to a squatting position and stared at Ezra like he and I were both dead and calmly waiting for whatever was to happen next.

"You have GOT to tell me what that felt like."

I was still smiling and spaced out and had barely said a thing when my mother stormed into the room, claiming that she had been calling for us for five minutes. Apparently Ezra's mother was in the car outside, pissed and waiting for him. And just like that, he was gone, with me still dazed on the floor and my mother looking at me with that what-the-hell-were-you-two-up-to look. I told my mom that we were just playing with Legos. I picked up some of the pieces that were under my butt. "Oof!" she said in her Israeli accent, then she shook her head and left me alone. And slowly, second by second, my world of worries came back. Another item on my list: the shame of my mother's disappointment.

As I sat there over dinner with my parents, listening to them talk about the latest tragedy in the Middle East, it was clear to me that there was only one thing to do. And so I started making a mental list of household items that could—without anyone's help—knock me unconscious.

Chapter Three
Righteous Room

Shmendrik and Ally are fabulous people. It's always fun when we go out with them. We drink. We laugh. We drink more. We laugh more. We can tell dirty secrets and dirty jokes and blur them all together until we've poured our hearts out like we've been blending one of my mother's gazpachos and it's two in the morning and we're not ready to leave the damn bar until they kick out the four crazy adults who are acting like they're seventeen.

I like seeing how much Julia cares about Shmen, even if sometimes it means tension about his drinking or his inability to hold onto a job, or my fear that, in his inebriation, he'll spill the *borscht* to Julia about our little low-interest, never-really-pay-back loan structure.

So, naturally, I'm resentful about going out with them when I could've been brooding alone at home with a blank piece of paper in front of me.

When we get to the Righteous Room, Shmen and Ally are, as usual, already there. There are four untouched martinis at the table. Hellos and kisses go all around, Julia admires Ally's sexy little boots, Ally admires Julia's hair, which gets longer and seems redder each time, I tell Shmen that he's getting too skinny, and Shmen tells me that I'm getting too bald. We each take sips of our martinis, a few words about the weather—

that crazy rain—and then Shmendrik points out that beside my glass and Julia's glass there are napkins with handwritten numbers on them. I have 12 and Julia has 10.

Shmen has to elbow Ally, who smiles in that shy way that she smiles, and then she explains Shmen's game to us. One number is the number of horses Ally has owned and the other is the number of men she's kissed. "That is," she says, "before I fell in love with this man," and she puts her arm around Shmen.

"You've got ten seconds to figure it out," Shmendrik tells us. And that's how the night begins.

#

Ally takes care of injured horses and brings them back to health for almost no pay. Imagine it: this skinny little woman calming a fifteen-hundred-pound horse. But this explains how she handles Shmen and her daughter, who both have more energy than a dozen injured horses.

It turns out that Ally has owned more horses than she has kissed men and that Shmen has had more surgeries than apples and that when Julia was a kid, she wrote 9 unanswered letters to Frank Sinatra and 7 to Johnny Cash. When it's my turn, I put the number 21 on a napkin and give it to Ally and then give the number 7 to Shmen. I say, "One number is the number of therapists I've had. The other is the number of lovers."

My wife sighs. "No brainer," she says, and she takes a sip of her drink.

#

The martinis are a thing I started. It's always gin, always straight up, always dry, always three olives. Not two, not one. Sometimes they pretend that they don't like this drink, especially my wife. She'll make a face, like it's a nasty medicine for a nasty disease, but I know she loves something about it. The hint of berry, the clean burn down the throat, and the pleasure of taking on a ritual that comes from a generation that is mostly just a shadow in our world. I got this habit from my father. That man drank at least one martini a day for fifty years. Toward the end of his life, when the doctor said he shouldn't drink so much, he began drinking even more, realizing that he didn't have much more time left to enjoy them. The martinis at the Righteous Room are good, though it took a little constructive guidance to get them to make it just right: be careful with the vermouth, dry off the olives first, don't let the gin sit too long in the shaker. My dad used to say that it's not hard to make a damn good martini, but it's damn easy to screw one up.

#

<u>drink 1</u>

Shmendrik explains to us about the dance he and Ally's daughter have learned. Shmen and Ally have been dating for less than two years, but her daughter fell in love with Shmen instantly.

"The trick," he says, "is to wave your clothes around in the air before you throw them at Mommy." He rubs Ally's back and Ally rolls her eyes while she drinks her martini. This is the life of Ally and Shmen. On paper, it sounds like Shmen is doing all the wrong things. But there's something about their family that's not on paper.

Julia says, "This sounds an awful lot like stripping."

"Oh," Shmen says. "It is." He puts his hand on his sister's hand. "But you have to understand, we don't take off our underwear."

Ally puts down her martini. "Yes you did," she says and gives him a punch in the shoulder.

"Oh yeah," he says. "I did."

#

<u>drink 2</u>

Ally tells me that a horse's instinct—even after an injury—is to keep running.

I say, "Really?" and I can see that she is trying to gauge whether I'm pulling her leg, this goofy Jew who is rarely serious, but her stories always do this to me. If I were dropped from an airplane right in the middle of Kansas, I'd barely be able to tell the difference between a horse and a cow and a pig, but sitting here in this bar listening to Ally talk, I can't get enough horse sense.

"Even when they break a bone in their leg," Ally tells me, "they'll run on it if you don't stop them."

And while I sit there learning about injured horses, I hear Shmen and Julia talk about Shmen's latest plan to get a psychology degree. Julia is always supportive even while she knows that he is unlikely to finish any degree. As long as I've known him, Shmen has always been halfway through a degree in something. Even though he has troubles following through with a degree, he reads like a monster and is able to say things like, "You can't read *Ulysses* for the third time until you've read it twice," and he can even make it sound funnier than it is arrogant. I'm supposedly the writer, but he's the one who is obsessed with language. He will call me at four in the morning to tell me that you can't spell "husband" without "anus."

#

It's one of those hipster bars we're in, with exposed pipes and exposed air vents, and I pretend that I'm up in the pipes rather than down here where all the regular people are. And from up in that maze of pipes, I can see Shmen, with his love of language, his love of obscure words and phrases, but without a clear plan to make use of this love, other than calling friends in the middle of the night. But then again, he might be the happiest man I know. And Julia. This is a woman who comes home after having a cigarette with an alcoholic who just died in her lap while apologizing to her because he thought she was his dead wife whom he had deceived for twenty-seven years. "Forgive me, Cassandra," this man kept saying to Julia, and Julia kept forgiving until the man finally died, and then, after this kind of day, Julia is still able to help me get my pants on and go out for drinks. This is also a woman who loves these fabulous masculine singers like Frank and Johnny and Elvis and then marries a scrawny little Jew who writes scrawny little stories. And there's Ally, who talks about such real-world things like listening to the heartbeat of a horse who has just broken his spine but still tries to get up. And while she speaks with such sympathy for this creature, I wonder if it's wrong of me to think: metaphor.

After savoring the metaphor for a while longer, I come down from the pipes to have another drink.

#

drink 3

"I just don't like the name," Ally says to me. She grabs my hand from across the table and squeezes it a little. She has a solid hold of me, and she looks me straight in the eyes.

"It's been a year now," she says. "And I still don't like it."

I don't know what she is talking about, but I enjoy her touch too much to ask.

Shmendrik starts massaging her neck. It makes them both seem so sweet. "The woman doesn't like the name you christened me," he says. "She thinks Shmendrik isn't appropriate."

"But it's perfect," I say.

"The word means fool," she says. "I looked it up. And it's a Yiddish word," she says. "Joel isn't a fool and he's got blonde hair and blue eyes."

"I know," I say. "That's why I love it."

Shmen smiles without talking, which is a rare sight, because he's always got something to say. Even when he has nothing to say, he's got something to say, and so I realize that this subject, for whatever reason, is a touchy one between them. Every relationship has an area that is tricky even if it has no right to be tricky—one of those arguments that seems ridiculous when you recount it to someone later, but somehow, at the time, it taps into something nasty. So I decide to keep my mouth shut and let Ally and Joel work it out, even though Joel totally doesn't look like a Joel—his own sister admits that.

"When Yuvi gets stuck on a name," Julia says, "there's nothing you can do about it." And then she lists off some of the people in our world that I've permanently named: our friend, Jason Shiffer, now known as Shiffer Brains; my disturbingly flirtatious aunt, known posthumously as Nafkeh; our postman, the Nazi.

Ally lets go of my hand and she looks seriously at Julia and me. Me and my wife, sitting there next to each other in the Righteous Room. Ally tries to size us up. I know from Shmen that she's an expert sizer-upper. This woman knows firsthand what a disaster a marriage can be and she's probably trying to understand where Julia and I fit into this spectrum. If we tease each other because we love each other or because we're hiding something.

And then Ally says to Julia, "Why hasn't he given you a name?"

#
<u>last call</u>

It's late into the night and Shmen is two to four drinks ahead of everyone else when he orders a gin and tonic to try and sober up.

The good-looking waiter with the gentile blue eyes keeps glancing over at my wife and I re-remember about that little note I found in her pocket. I had forgotten about it for hours, but the dread inside of me has returned. The contractions are getting more frequent and I wonder how much longer I can carry this napkin inside of me.

Julia says, "How you feeling, Shmen?"

I've seen Julia's pretty freckly face get more serious the more drinks Shmen orders. Between Shmen's little digestive disease and the way their mother drank when she was alive, it isn't easy for Julia to watch him drink like that.

"Great," Shmen says. "I feel like a million dollars' worth of intestinal surgery."

I press my hand on Julia's thigh. I squeeze it and feel the tightness in her muscles.

"Let's quit drinking," she suggests. "I think it's enough."

"For you or for me?" he asks and doesn't look her in the eyes.

It's about ten seconds of silence at the table until Ally says, "Actually, I think I'm ready to go home myself. We still have to take the babysitter home."

And that's how tension inflates and deflates with a Protestant family. Not that I'm the prototype for direct communication, with all my secrets and fears and worries, my inability to write even the first page of a novel, all the ways I have of joking around any problem, how I can turn a concern about the stability of my marriage into a discussion about whether I should wear the beige pants to dinner, how I can suggest that we hold off serious discussions until the tensions in the Middle East are over.

Before we leave that night, Julia and Shmen give each other hugs that last too long and I hear Julia say "I love you" to her brother and I hear her brother say to his only sibling, "You're one of my favorite older sisters."

Ally and Shmen leave the bar first. Shmen is limping. It's something I've noticed over the weeks—not quite a limp as much as a hint of a limp—and I hadn't consciously thought about it until just now. Even so, I don't say anything about it to Julia.

"Let's go, honey," she says to me. "You're looking far too happy."

LOVERS AND THERAPISTS

My first girlfriend told me that she loved me more than anyone else in the whole world. My first therapist told me I was incapable of love but that I should keep a journal of my emotions.

My second girlfriend told me that I could give her a hotter orgasm than anyone in the world. My second therapist told me that my emotional growth was stunted at the oral phase of development and that I should find out if I was breastfed.

My third girlfriend loved how I stayed up as late as she did even though I had class so early in the morning. My third therapist told me that I had to get on medication so I could finally get some sleep.

My fourth girlfriend told me that she loved doing happy hour with me. My fourth, fifth, six, and ninth therapists told me that I had a drinking problem.

My fifth girlfriend told me that she really enjoyed our alone time. My fifteenth therapist told me that I needed to get out more.

My sixth girlfriend told me that I'm a coward, especially in the bedroom. My eighteenth therapist told me that I had narcissistic personality disorder but that I also had nice, full lips.

My wife tells me that I'm the most insecure person she's ever met. My twenty-first therapist tells me to reconsider my writing career.

Chapter Four
Getting Wet

I keep the window open as my wife drives us home so I can feel the specks of drizzle against my arm. It feels like it's been drizzling for years. I'm glad Julia loves to drive, because I'd rather get another circumcision than drive at night, in the rain, under the influence of however many martinis.

Even in my real life, I lose track of the plot. I can never remember names or places or details. I have no idea whether to turn left or right. I don't know what time we arrived or what time we left. All I remember is how everyone felt when whatever happened happened. And even if nothing happens, it still feels to me like something happened. "*Oof!*" my mom used to say when I was a kid, "you care too much about how everyone feels. *Hakol Beseder*. It's all okay. If you don't relax, you'll be dead before you can help anyone anyway."

I wave my arm up and down in the windy rain until Julia says, "Roll the window up. We're getting wet."

"But I'm having a poignant moment," I say to her.

"Have your poignant moment while I'm still dry."

Julia pats my thigh a few times and it's a sweet enough gesture for me to forget about how much we sound like a mother and son and so I roll up the window.

Julia doesn't talk much about her mother and her father, but I know how those two are deep inside her. And I know that she watches her brother carefully for the signs. Whether he'll turn into the vicious mess of their father or the catatonic mess of their mother. And I know she grows tired of me and my insecurities. She is tired of how I look at every gorgeous man on the street with the quiet threat that he might be the one to steal my wife from me—as if my wife has no say in the matter. And she is worried about her own aspirations, whether we can really afford this nonprofit project that she is taking on alongside my overdue-contractual-obligation of a career, whether our rainy day fund can last through a rainy season that seems to be going on forever.

I say to Julia, "I really like your brother."

"Me too," she says.

It's a rare moment. There's no humor in our words. There's no irony or sarcasm. It's not a quote from a Woody Allen film. There are no secrets underneath what we say out loud.

If there's anything underneath, it's a mutual worry about her brother's health. Protestants sometimes act like they're invincible. Jews, we're nothing if not for our diseases and how we talk about them.

Her brother has a disease that is more commonly found in Jewish genes. In my own twisted way, I feel both honored and guilt-ridden about this fact, this kid from Iowa with a Mediterranean disease. But I don't talk about his health much to Julia because I know Julia's invincible Protestant *tuches* will kick my weak Semitic *tuches* if I talk about it as much as I want to talk about it. So I talk about nothing—*shtuyot*, as my mom called it.

"For you," I say, "it doesn't count as much to like him, because you two are related."

"No," she tells me. "Related makes it even more impressive."

I sometimes forget: this is a woman who didn't even go to her father's funeral.

Even though I once pegged myself as a lousy secret keeper, I've gotten shamefully good. It started out as helping her brother pay one late gas bill that he was too ashamed to talk to Julia about, and by the end of the year, I had paid for a transmission for his car and two surgeries for his intestines and now I'm the one too scared to tell Julia.

But under the influence of a few martinis, I want to tell her about it. I want to tell her everything. Spill my intestines out on the dashboard and see where that takes us. We could even clean up the mess with cocktail napkins that have messages on them from all her beautiful, muscular, non-balding, gentile lovers. But I'm sober enough to realize that I'm too scared to let out so much of my intestines. "Don't be such a coward," she once said to me over a game of Monopoly when I wouldn't buy Marvin Gardens.

She was right about Marvin Gardens.

I say to my wife, "I should write a story about Shmen and Ally."

"Don't write about my brother," she says, even though she doesn't need to say anything with how tightly she is squeezing my thigh.

"No," I explain, "I can write it from Ally's perspective. With that scientific mind of hers. It would be fun. I bet she has an interesting story to tell. And I'd like to show how good Shmen is with the kid."

And then Julia squeezes my thigh even tighter.

I start thinking seriously about their story. I start thinking how much I'd like to tell it, if only for a few pages. But Julia still doesn't let go of my thigh.

Julia looks over at me and then back at the blurry road. "I've been thinking," she says, "about a baby."

"You mean the constipated one next door that drools on everything?"

"Have you thought about a baby?"

"No," I say. It's not exactly the truth and it's not exactly a lie. The truth is that I *have* thought about a baby, and I've decided that it's something I don't want to think about. Even saying the word "baby" is something I can't handle for at least another couple dozen martinis. Not tonight. Maybe not in my lifetime.

She lets go of my thigh. I hear that familiar sound of her blowing the frustrated air out of her mouth.

It's a typical situation for me: the plot gets too twisted too quickly and now I can't find my way out.

Or even worse: I can't find a way in.

I roll the window down, just a crack, to get some fresh air.

"Yeah," I say. "I should really write a story about Shmen and Ally."

I LOVE THE WAY YOU POOP WHEN YOU POOP WITH ME

If I told you the fact that my boyfriend and my seven-year-old daughter performed a strip show in the living room—swinging their shirts in the air before throwing them at each other—you'd probably get the wrong impression.

#

FACT: The average human colon is five and a half feet long and is composed of four main sections: the sigmoid, the descending, the transverse, and the ascending.

#

It's morning. We're at my boyfriend's apartment. My boyfriend and I are fooling around in bed when he sees the time and realizes that he needs to get ready for his job interview. We're usually too busy to fool around, but not the kind of busy that brings in money.

#

FACT: My boyfriend is five and a half feet tall. He has no colon. He lives on the third floor of a six-story apartment complex. He's not good at keeping jobs.

#

My boyfriend grabs three shirts on hangers from the closet. He holds one shirt in each hand and hangs one on his erection and says, "Honey, which of these three do you prefer?"

#

FACT: I have my daughter from Thursdays to Sundays and her father gets her the rest of the week. Today is Saturday and, while my boyfriend hangs a shirt on his cock, my daughter is in the living room, which we converted into her bedroom.

#

My daughter doesn't like the apartment where I live. She says it's boring. She always wants to go to my boyfriend's apartment instead. I feel the same way, and we do spend most of our time at his place, but I often argue on the side of my apartment because it feels wrong not to stand up for where I'm from.

#

My daughter said that my boyfriend is down to earth. I said, "What do you mean down to earth? Where did you get those words from?" She said, "You know, he treats me like a regular person. And he's good at freeze tag." I thought to say, "Too bad freeze tag doesn't pay fifteen or twenty bucks an hour."

#

My daughter is awake. I hear her singing from the other room. She's changed the lyrics to her favorite pop song so that it goes like this: "I love the way you poop when you poop with me."

#

FACT: Before I knew him, my boyfriend went into the hospital on thirty-one occasions during the two years that he was sick before the big surgery.

#

I tell my boyfriend that it's his fault that my daughter is always talking about poop. My boyfriend blames his affection for words like poop on his lack of a colon. It's "poop envy," he explains.

#

FACT: My boyfriend has what is known as a "J Pouch." Through the magic of surgery, they reconnected his insides so that his small intestine now has a pouch in it to mimic his missing colon. The only problem is that he has to go to the bathroom a lot. When things get inflamed in there, which happens every few months, it's called "pouchitis" and it makes bathroom visits less than pleasant for him. "Another case of the itis," he'll tell me.

#

My boyfriend told me that the nurses would come visit him even after their shift, that they would play cards and joke for hours with him. My boyfriend's parents never understood why overworked nurses would stick around the hospital like that, playing hearts with my boyfriend.

#

My daughter has no patience for board games but will play with a deck of cards for hours. She wanted to know why one king had a knife in his head. I thought to say that it was because the queen caught him cheating on her but then my boyfriend said that it was because nobody would let the guy poop. I'm glad he spoke up first.

#

FACT: My daughter's father slept with a blonde blackjack dealer when my daughter was one year old. I didn't find out for another year. We didn't divorce for another year.

#

FACT: In the last interview, my boyfriend was asked what his weaknesses were, and he told the guy that he was lazy and sleepy and had digestive problems and that he was a bit of a drunk. Then he made the drinky drinky motion. He didn't get the job.

#

My boyfriend's disease is not getting better. Sometimes, while he is in the bathroom trying to deal with the inflammation and scar tissue deep inside of him, I cry in the bedroom, begging for a simpler life. When he comes out of the bathroom, he always has a smile on his face, like he was just awarded some kind of prize. It makes me angry that he isn't more upset.

\#

FACT: I have a picture of my boyfriend and my daughter doing push-ups. Except that their pants are pulled down so you can see both their butts. One is bony and hairy. One is cute and chunky. It's true that I was amused enough to take the picture, but it was my boyfriend who put it on the fridge door.

\#

My mother was horrified at the sight of this picture. I tried to explain to her that it was all in good fun. That my boyfriend is as sweet as any adult has ever been to my daughter. But my mother didn't look my boyfriend in the eyes all through dinner.

\#

Before he leaves the room, my boyfriend is looking good with his tie and his shiny shoes. He gives me a kiss and tickles me in those places he knows about. I can hear a grumble in his stomach and I know it'll be hard for him to last through the interview without running to the bathroom. When he walks away from me, I see that he is limping slightly—even though he denies it.

\#

On his way out of the room, I say, "Break a leg," and he comes crashing down on the hardwood floor of the living room. I suspect that he fell harder than his joke intended. But my daughter is clapping and giggling from the other room.

\#

FACT: My daughter loves that man.

\#

When I first kissed him, it was on the balcony of a friend's place. We were the only two people outside because the keg was inside and outside was cold and windy. He whispered in my ear, "It's not true to say that I don't want to entertain the idea of not avoiding something with you." He looked at me with his lips and eyes smiling and not smiling. It's magic that way he can hold onto something sweet in a mess of crazy. He was so soft about how he touched my cheek with two fingers and then held my neck and kissed me on the lips. But I started to laugh and he didn't separate from me. He laughed too, with our lips still together like that, and then we stopped laughing, and we were just breathing again, but with our lips together, not really kissing. Just breathing.

#

Even back then, he warned me that he had a nasty little disease, that he was up to his ears in debt from all that scar tissue. But back then, I didn't care, because he was so lovely. And now, I do care, because he is so lovely.

Chapter Five
Restraint

It's three in the morning and it feels like forever since we were out with Shmen and Ally, even though it was only a few hours ago. Julia and I are both awake (at opposite ends of the house) when I start thinking about the nylon restraints in the bottom drawer of my desk.

I love these nights when the rain is so hard you think you can feel it thrashing in your temples. Julia's been doing paperwork in the living room and I've been reading and re-reading an Isaac Bashevis Singer story in my office. Julia is getting ready to start her own nonprofit that helps families affected by alcoholism and I'm trying to figure out how the son of the rabbi in this story is able to stare at a sexy woman's legs for so many paragraphs. Does Singer get away with it because of the boy or because of the legs?

When we got married, we both agreed that babies were not on our radar. The idea of someone depending on me while I walk around in my underwear not writing sounds too terrifying to think about. I'd rather keep my failures to myself.

My editor suggested that I amp up the tension in my stories to make them more interesting. "You know," she says. "Put a birth or a death in there. Put a murder in the story. Or even better, connect your story to the struggles of Israel and Palestine." I think about this for a good long moment. It's true that I've got Israeli blood inside of me, but I don't know how to write about a seemingly hopeless struggle where no one is speaking the same language. So I say to my editor, "Fine. Send me the complete manuscript you want me to write."

I'm desperate to do anything other than confront my novel. I'll write page after page of poop stories about my brother-in-law to avoid my novel. So far, my novel is about nothing. It's about worse than nothing: it's about not being able to write. I start making clawing gestures with my hands and I know it's a sign that it's not going to be a great night.

I miss my father, and I haven't even told his story yet. He's in plenty of my short stories and essays, but I can't show you those. Because I'm a novelist. Or a faux-novelist. A fauxvelist. So you don't know how I felt about that man—that man who died without a prostate and with stents in his arteries and with enough fly rods to build a cathedral.

It's another of my failings.

I keep expecting my wife to bug me about something, you know, about the bills or needing to get to bed or needing to check that the gutters aren't clogged or if I'm hungry or needing help with some of the accounting, but she hasn't checked on me in two hours. I can still hear papers shuffling, imagine her with those reading glasses on, doing research about 401c's or 407d's or 501k's…I'm dying for her to bug me about something. Anything. Almost anything.

I can't stop thinking about the words on that napkin: Save Me, Julia. If it weren't written in someone else's handwriting on someone else's napkin, then I would have suspected myself of writing it.

Julia and I sometimes pretend that we have little affection for each other, but when we eventually make our way to the bed, when we get too sleepy to keep our guard up, we do slowly, eventually, end up close to each other, maybe holding hands, maybe a little deep-sleep spooning, or maybe we sleep for an hour with my lips against her back, or her arm around my waist. But as it gets close to morning again, we separate, go back to opposite sides of the bed. And when we wake up, we're back to our protected selves. That's how it goes with us.

But even with our guard up, we have an understanding about each other's needs. There are some things needed just for survival. So I open my drawer, the bottommost drawer, and pull out the nylon restraints I bought at a sex shop a few years ago. I take off all my clothes. Then I remember about the scabs on my ass that I don't want her to see. Because I supposedly stopped doing those kinds of things. So I put my boxers back on. And then I fasten the nylon straps to each arm and each leg, making sure the Velcro fasteners are nice and tight. I grab the rest of the equipment that she'll use to strap me to the bed. I grab my wife's leather belt from the bedroom. And I make my trek to the living room.

Maybe these big rainstorms only come when you're trying to work something out inside yourself—something big about who you are or what you believe in. And they don't let up until you've made some kind of movement. In my narcissism, I wonder if this rainstorm is trying to tell me something.

The metal hooks on the restraints make little clicking sounds as I walk. Which causes my wife to turn around and see me standing there like a horny little *golem*—standing there naked with restraints and her belt. She is deep into her work and it takes some time for her to take in the situation. If there is a message in this rainstorm, then I hope I can still receive it while being handcuffed to the bedpost and spanked.

My wife takes a deep breath. My poor wife; I know she isn't crazy about doing these things to me. She wants regular sex like in the early days of our marriage. But I can't give that to her right now. Shame is all that turns me on these days.

Save Me, Julia.

"Do you need to be taught a lesson?" she asks me with the seriousness of someone who's been doing tedious accounting.

I love those reading glasses of hers.

The wind blows hard. The rain bangs against the window. Even indoors, it seems that we should be wearing raincoats, that we need protection from all that we're up against.

TALKING TO GOD

When I was six years old, I had a vivid picture in my mind that God was dressed in a thick yellow raincoat with a yellow rain hat shaped like an origami boat. I don't know where this image came from, but it was something I was sure of. And so, I felt blessed one afternoon when Mom and I were sitting on the front steps of our apartment, after that vicious rainstorm, and I saw a tall man in just that outfit coming toward us. The sky had cleared up in a matter of minutes and the sun was shining bright, even with the ground still wet. The yellow of his raincoat was the purest yellow I could imagine. His bangs were thick and curly and completely gray. He had a limp in his walk, but it also made him pop up with every other step in a way that seemed more certain than typical walking.

My mother wasn't looking at him, she was looking out at the parking lot. I think we were waiting for someone to pick us up for some event, a birthday party or a trip to the mall. I tugged on my mother's sweater—she often wore thick sweaters with a lot of material to grab. She leaned toward me and said, "What is it, mameleh?" in her gentle voice. She used Hebrew words instead of English for all the warmest and coldest things.

I tried to be subtle about the way I pointed in the man's direction. He was getting closer and humming a tune and he made little coughs at the high notes. I asked my mother, "Is he God?"

"What?" my mother said. She was smiling, already knew her son was about to say something she'd be amused by.

I said, "Is the man in the raincoat Adonai?"

My mother looked at me, then she looked at this man—he was almost in front of us—and then she looked back at me, and then she looked back at the man. I figured that my mother was sincerely considering this insight of mine.

The man stopped in front of us, as if we had called for him. I was sure that he knew exactly what we had been speaking about—an easy thing for God to know.

"What is it, Tziona?" the man said. I didn't know at the time that my mom had already met this man before, that this man was a neighbor of ours. His voice had a scratchiness that made me think he was very wise—rather than that he had smoked two packs a day for forty years.

I still believed this man was God, but I also had the feeling that if my mother revealed my question to this man, it would destroy whatever power I had given him.

My mother looked down at me one last time. I'm sure I had some kind of desperation on my face, and then she looked back up at our neighbor, David Watts. "My son asked me if you are God."

David put his hand above his eyes to block the glare of the sun and gave me a good look. "You want to know if I am... God?"

Both of them—Mom and David—had that gut-busting kind of laugh; they were clutching their stomachs from the pain, wiping the tears from their faces. This was one hell of a moment. I wanted to get away from the two of them but my body wouldn't move. I couldn't even manage to cover my face with my hands. I was stuck there watching.

After a few minutes of this, David scratched my head forcefully, messed up my hair that way I hated, and then he limped away, coughing and laughing at the same time. When he was nearly out of sight, I heard him say, "Goddamn, that's a great line. I'll have to remember that one."

I vowed never to say anything personal to my mother again. I regretted everything important I ever told her. The wind started blowing and I remember being cold, sitting there in the wet sunny weather.

My mom put her arm around me. She tried to shake me in a playful way. But when she saw that I wouldn't budge, she squeezed me instead. She put her lips to my forehead—they were warm and moist—and she said so that it vibrated right through my forehead, "It's okay, mameleh."

And just like that, I was glad to be going to the mall with my mother.

Chapter Six
Noah

My wife unhooks me from the bed and says, "I hope that did the trick."

It did. It's the closest thing that we have to sex these days. She's got all her clothes on and I'm in my boxers with my ass burning from all that spanking. Not one orgasm within a five-mile radius of our bedroom.

Julia isn't looking at me; she's looking out the dark window. She is trying to decide if she can do more work or if it's time to finally get to bed. She needs to have a business plan together by the end of the week. I shouldn't have interrupted her work.

It's still raining and it feels like the rain has gone on for too long. I think of saying something about how we're like Noah and his wife, but I already know how that conversation goes. We're not the best example of the male and female of the species. And I haven't read anywhere about Noah having a predilection for being spanked by his wife.

"It's not normal," she says to the window.

I rub my wrists to get the blood circulating again. "The rain has been going on for too long," I say.

"I'm talking about you," she says. "When are we going to have normal sex again? It's been three years. I don't like doing this stuff to you."

"It's not my fault," I tell her. What I want to tell her is that it is my fault. That somehow everything feels like my fault and I want to be punished for it all. That I can't imagine normal sex with her because when we're pressed up against each other, all I think about are the things that are wrong in our lives. Like that other man who writes her messages on napkins and sticks them in her pants.

I track down a pair of pants from the closet. It's strange putting on a fresh pair at four in the morning. "It's not my fault," I say again, with my pants on I feel more comfortable deflecting, "the problem has to do with mistakes made by the government."

"If you blame the Bush administration one more time," my wife says, "I will never tie you up again."

It's true. I love to blame the Bush administration. They did so many things wrong—why not tack on a little problem of sexual intimacy? At one point in my life, I blamed my father for all my problems. But I got over it. Besides, my father had charm. That's more than what you could say for the Bush administration.

It's red around Julia's eyes and her hair is messy and she sighs a little too much. Her lips move slightly but I know she isn't about to say anything. She's got her hand buried inside her hair and she scratches her scalp to get the itch out.

"You're getting crazier than the characters in your stories," she says.

I take a deep breath. I try to relax. What we need is one of those coming-to-Jesus moments. I've always wanted a coming-to-Jesus moment. Non-believers deserve them too. And I can tell that Julia and I need to get back on track somehow. It didn't used to be this crooked with us.

I say, "Julia. Do you want the real story? Do you want the whole *megillah*?" And I prepare myself for something that I'm not exactly prepared for.

She takes a deep breath. She tries to relax. She closes her eyes. I can see her eyeballs moving underneath as if she were asleep. And when she opens her eyes again, she says, "I'm sorry. Not tonight," and then steps out of the room with her leather belt and her exasperation, leaving me alone on the bed with my disappointment and my relief.

MATCHBOX CARS AND RAINBOW TROUT

I was bouncing up and down on the hotel bed, banging matchbox cars into each other. I was making too much noise in too small a room on too ugly a day. I knew it was wrong, but it was a strange moment for me—I had seen tears in my dad's eyes for the first time ever—so jumping on the bed and banging cars seemed as good a way as any to pass the time until things returned to normal.

He almost never hit me; his anger mostly circled in the realm of nasty words and nasty eyes. But those eyes were big and brown and bloodshot. And this was the day of his mother's funeral, with me jumping on the bed and banging cars together and yelling "Deathtrap!" whenever two cars crashed into each other.

I'm not saying that I deserved it, but if he were ever going to lose control, this was as good a day as any. His belt flew off his waist so fast I could hear it cut through the air. It was made of three intertwined pieces of leather and made a web-like pattern on my thigh. I was crying instantly, just as instantly as my dad stormed out of the hotel room (his belt still on the bed), just as instantly as my mom was at my side, holding my hand, saying, "It's okay, mameleh. It's okay, darling." With her Israeli accent, darling sounded like dahling, which still seems to me a far sweeter word.

\#

In my twenties, I started cutting myself. Little slits on my chest, on my arm, sometimes on my hip exactly where the waistband of my boxers would chafe as I walked. On my ass, so that every time I sat down I would remember. I loved feeling that burn during the worst days of my depression. "But you have nothing to be depressed about," is what my friends would tell me. So I stopped talking to my friends. They didn't understand how I burned, feeling inadequate and unloved no matter what I did. I learned how to cut myself, how to stare at the blood in the mirror at three in the morning, and then to sit back and relax to a Simpsons episode, ideally a season five or six episode, when the writers figured out how to get the best out of the characters, but before they got desperate for a story.

#

When my father hit me that day, I cried, but there was relief in the smack as well. Usually, there was just that rage in his eyes and in his words, and since we never spoke of it, and since he never apologized, it was hard to know if it was real. Our arguments became blurred dreams afterward, vague enough that I sometimes thought I made them up. Except on the morning he hit me—I had this beautiful bruise right on my thigh. It was as many colors as the skin of a fish when you looked at it in the right light.

My dad came back to the room after an hour. Nobody spoke. My parents prepared for the funeral, I stayed in the room with a babysitter, and they were off, the belt still on the bed.

When we returned home to Atlanta, he bought me the exact three matchbox cars that I wanted—even the hard-to-find one with the black widow spider on the hood, that red hourglass mark showing on its abdomen.

This smack of the belt was not a pivotal event for me. One smack isn't such a messy thing for a child to overcome if you think about how much worse it could be. He had good days and he had bad days, just like anyone else.

It was two dozen years later, when I was thirty-four and he was seventy-six, that my father spoke to me about this event, which I had nearly forgotten. Imagine my father at seventy-six: that gray beard, those long bony arms, with my mother dead, his sister dead, most of his friends dead, after his open heart surgery, after surviving cancer, after he turned to fly fishing like a religion.

I was already living in Portland, but I still came to visit him in North Carolina twice a year. He had moved back to the area where he grew up—the Pisgah National Forest. During these trips, we spent the mornings outdoors, then came back home in the afternoon for a martini or two, depending on how he felt that day. He brought up the day in the hotel while we were walking along the Davidson River. It was his favorite stretch, where you could walk down to the water and step right in if you wanted.

"Come on," my father said, and waved me into the water. He was wearing a pair of tennis shoes older than me. It was the first time I noticed how little hair he had on his legs, and I wondered when that change had happened. His movements were not of the fragile man I thought him to be. He stepped with ease on rocks that were covered in slippery moss, never lost balance.

I was wearing my favorite black pair of shoes, but I followed him into the water anyhow.

It was so cold at first I had to squeeze my eyes shut. But after a few seconds, the pain went away and it felt more like a tickle. I started walking in the river.

"We need a good rain," he said loud enough for me to hear him downstream, and he squatted to touch the water. He put his wet fingers up to his nose. My father, smelling the river.

"It feels so good in the water," I said. It was strange to walk into a river, it seemed wrong and freeing, like driving around without a seatbelt. The water was shallow—barely up to my ankles—but it was moving fast and I had a continuous feeling that I was about to fall.

"I tell people," my father yelled back to me, "that the only reason I fish is to have an excuse to be standing knee deep in a river."

I made my way with awkward steps up to where my father was squatting and I squatted next to him. He had a small rock in his hand and he turned it over, as if reading its backside. He said, "I never forgave myself for hitting you after my mama died."

It took me a few moments to recollect what happened in that room. I remembered my father crying about his mother and the way he covered his eyes with his bony fingers—and then I remembered the belt on the bed, and that bruise on my thigh. As I watched my father turn that rock over and over, I understood how many times my father had replayed that scene in his head, how many times he regretted what happened with the belt.

"Hell," he said. He threw his little rock upstream as far as he could throw it. "It all seems so easy when you're sitting in the middle of a river."

I looked down at the water and said nothing. As we squatted there, I was struggling not to fall over, but my father was firmly planted. He reached over and rubbed my back and massaged my neck. It made me feel safe the way it did when I was a kid, even though it became that much harder to keep my balance.

And then, as if someone had called to him, my dad stood up. And so I stood up as well, looking and listening for signs. All I could hear was the river.

Upstream, I could see a big rock against the shore. From where we stood, the rock looked so much like a grand piano that I wondered if someone had carved into it to make this effect.

"I like to stand on that rock," my father said, "and fish into the water just below. They love wooly buggers down there in Piano Pond."

I thought of him standing there, so tall on that piano.

"You know," my father said, "when I wake up in the morning, all I pray for is to be able to get out on the river one more time."

He kept looking at that rock, squinting as if he could almost make out a person playing it. But the more I looked at the rock, the more it just looked like a rock.

"You got a lousy deal that day," he said. "I wish I could take it back."

I wanted to reach out to him so badly. To say something. Even if I conjured up a cliché, it would have felt better than saying nothing. Even now, as I sit at my computer 2,200 miles away from that river, I'm still trying to make the memory of myself say something to my father, just one truth about how I felt about him.

#

The first time Julia caught me cutting myself, my pants and underwear were on the floor, and I was standing on the bathroom counter, my ass toward the medicine cabinet mirror. I had a razor in my hand.

I don't remember what I was worried about that day, but it was surely something catastrophic and forgettable.

I pressed the razor hard against my ass and slid the razor vertically so that the blade had a chance to make long, continuous contact with my skin. I did this several times in a row. At first, there was no visible mark. But there was a beautifully sharp pain that tingled from my ass to my head to my toes. There were twenty or more seconds before the blood finally rose to the surface. And then they appeared: those gorgeous, bright red lines across the flesh.

When a wife enters the house expecting to surprise her husband with his favorite lunch (pastrami on rye from Zook's Deli), it is not a fabulous feeling for her to see her husband balancing on the bathroom counter with streaks of blood across his ass.

She covered her mouth with her hand. And through her skinny fingers she said, "What in God's name." She wouldn't look up at me at first, just down at the floor, where my pants were, where my feet should have been planted. And then she looked up.

It took that look in her eyes for me to know how abnormal this situation was. It sure felt like a normal thing to do on a day when my writing wasn't going well or when I missed my father or when the mailman was annoyed with me about our rickety mailbox.

I told her that I wouldn't cut myself again. That was three years ago. When I stopped cutting, I lost the ability to have sex with her—a notable side effect. Even though I've started cutting myself again, the other problems still haven't gotten better. Things have only gotten worse, because now I feel guilty about cutting on top of all the other things.

When I climbed down from the counter, I noticed drops of blood by the sink. Bright and rounded like little ladybugs. I was careful not to smudge them.

I stood there in the bathroom, pantsless, looking at Julia. She didn't say anything and I didn't say anything. But I still waited—it was easy to make eye contact with her, even though her eyes were searching all over the room for something besides eye contact with me. Pretty soon, she walked away.

I loved doing this cutting ritual and I knew it would be hard to let go of. It was something that was in me to love long before that one little moment when my father hit me with that belt and then bought me a black widow matchbox car to make up for it.

The matchbox car is still with me—in a shoebox in my closet. The two front wheels are missing, and the back wheels are too bent to spin. Sometimes, when I'm looking for something to be sentimental about, I squeeze the cold metal of the little car and think about how many years a man can carry around the things of his past.

#

It was my father who saw it first. He tapped me gently on the shoulder and pointed down by our feet. Almost nibbling at our toes was a rainbow trout. Maybe a foot long, shining from the light of the sun. It was too big and bright for this dull little river. We kept as still as we possibly could. The fish wiggled silently up to us. It inspected my father's feet and then my feet, and after careful consideration, it made a quick turn upstream.

"There's been a mayfly hatch," my father said. He took a deep breath, as if he could smell insect larvae. This was my father's world. I was just a visitor here, but he was as natural to this river as the water itself.

The fish swam out of sight in less than a second but we stood there quietly for five minutes. Maybe we were expecting the fish to come back to us. Or maybe we were trying to say goodbye.

Chapter Seven
Palindrome

It's nearly dawn when the phone rings. I grab it and take it out of the bedroom before picking up.

"Hello?" I say.

"It's Shmen. What's up?"

Whenever the phone rings at night, I first think that it's my father, that something has happened to him, or my mother, calling from Israel, that there's been an emergency with life or death at stake. Even now that they're dead, the reflex won't go away.

Shmen double-checks about borrowing some money. I say, "Of course," and then he tells me his latest palindrome.

When I come back to the bed, Julia asks me who it was.

"Wrong number," I say.

"Liar," she says in a groggy whisper muffled by her pillow.

It's our usual ritual when Shmen calls at night. I lie. She accuses. It shows love, even though I can't explain to you how.

My ass burns from the cuts I gave myself earlier, followed by all that spanking. And now that insane palindrome of his is chattering in my head. Between the burn and the chattering, I feel terrible. I can't keep one coherent thought in my head. So now maybe I can finally get some sleep.

I, madam, I made bone of live flesh.
Ah self, evil foe, no bed!
Am I mad?
Am I?

Book 2

EXODUS

Chapter Eight
A Brilliant Novel in the Works

She's been working more. Her organization is just getting off the ground. She has thirty-seven volunteers in just three months helping thirty-two alcoholics in twenty-nine families of need. She believes that it's not about alcoholism, it's about hopelessness. How's that for an impossible-sounding task: to instill hope. I'd rather try to rip someone's colon out through their ear. She's been on the local radio. She even has a catchy mission statement with sincere nouns like "community" and "generosity" in it. And while she generously helps the community, I spend my time thinking thoughts like: She could be humping any member of this generous community while I sit at home like an idiot.

I try to write. I have a novel that is a steaming pile of personal essays with no plot except one about an author who has no idea how to write a novel. And that is how it looks on the very best of days. My editor is frustrated with me as if she expected so much more out of me. And I want to please her. I tell her that I just need to do a little more research.

"Research what?" she asks.

In my research, I've found out that two blue Xanax pills take me from dangerously antsy to too antsy. And that three pills take me to very antsy and that four pills take me to a nap. Vicodin shoots me through the whole antsy spectrum and lands me smack in the middle of a brilliant apathy. Followed by a monstrous headache.

In my research, I've also found that staring at the baby pictures of Julia does not help my antsiness. It makes me long even more for something that I do not have.

The good news is that Julia's busyness has replaced any talk of her wanting a baby. Which simplifies my worries and failings to less than forty-five line items.

It's ten in the morning on a Tuesday, and while I'm sitting at my desk, I hear the lock on the front door clicking. Then there's the sound of someone breaking into the house. It's a murderer, I decide. Someone has come to rob my house and kill me. My first thought: poor intruder, they'll hardly find anything of value in this house. I can't even sell my own books, so what is the murderer going to do with them?

The murderer is getting closer to me. I hear heels clicking against the hardwood floor. And then the murderer steps into my office.

"Jesus," the murderer says. "You've been in nothing but that same pair of underwear for a week now. This place smells like rotten coffee grinds. I think you've gone three steps past stir crazy."

The murderer is in that beautiful black dress that I bought her a year ago. The one that looks abominably wrinkled in a way that only she could make sexy. I knew it would be great on her before she even tried it on. She's shaved her legs today. I see the eyeliner. And that long red hair that only gets redder.

"My brother wants to meet you for lunch," the murderer says. "Get the hell out of this house for a change."

It's gotten heartbreaking to see her these days. I fake naps and fake writing just to avoid her. I tell her that it's the novel that is killing me.

But it's her.

Or the things I find in her pants.

Our communication skills are at an all-time low. We've created a new language just to avoid talking about what we need to talk about. I'm tempted to tell her about the failed sign language I created as a kid. But that would involve communicating with her.

"You've got to get your act together," she tells me.

"Hush, woman!" I say to her. "There's a brilliant novel in the works!" And then I close the door and call the murderer's brother.

SIGN LANGUAGES

My fifth grade class at the Hebrew Academy was unusually imbalanced. Out of the thirty students in our grade, there were only two girls. Our whole grade was stunted by the imbalance. No one thought to approach these girls in a "going out with a girl" kind of way even though our counterparts at the nearby public school had moved on to kissing and touching and even a few isolated stories of going all the way.

Recess at our school was kickball and jungle gyms and playing on the swings and capture the flag and hopscotch. It was trading stickers and trading baseball cards. Getting in trouble for picking on the younger kids. Running away from the older kids. But for Ezra and me, it was hiding behind the four biggest pine trees in the back of the field and talking about girls. Both of them. It turned out that Ezra liked Shayna Eisenberg better and I liked Nari Tanaka better.

"I daydream about her all the time," he said to me. "I think about her naked all the time. I touch her boobs over and over and over and then I take off all her clothes and then we do it. I can't stop thinking about doing it. I'm dying to do it."

Ezra was smacking his hand on the bark of the tree as he told this to me and pieces of bark fell to the ground.

"I know exactly what you mean," I said to him, even though I had no idea what he meant. It wasn't that my daydreams were way different than his, but they were different. I didn't dream about doing it. I dreamed that Nari would strip me to my underwear, that she'd tie me up, that she'd throw me face down

*on the ground and then step on me with her dirty tennis shoes
and then sit on me as I lay there helpless and begging for her to
stop, with her butt cheeks rubbing on my spine. She'd explain
all the ways that I had misbehaved. If I had enough time in my
fantasy, perhaps we'd eventually get to the point where she'd put
her hand in my underwear, and sometime after that, maybe
she'd take off her clothes too, maybe I'd touch her once in a while,
and there was an off chance that we might eventually do it. But
I rarely got past the excitement of her strength and my shame.
So I said to Ezra, "Yeah. I think about doing it all the time too."*

*"We've got to do something about it," he said, looking at the
bark all over the ground.*

*With all this excitement about these two girls, Ezra and I did
what any two boys would do in a lopsided, Jewish elementary
school when they liked two girls. We formed a group of only
boys and created a fully formed sign language to discuss these
girls behind their backs.*

#

*Our sign language was a disaster. The only functional part
of the language was that holding up one finger in the air
represented Shayna, and two fingers meant Nari. But we also
had signs for more than a hundred words plus every letter of
the alphabet. And as much as we tried to train everyone in the
group, it never worked the way we wanted it to. For example, in
the middle of class, I'd want to tell Ezra that I could see Nari's
black underwear when I dropped my pencil on the floor and
went to pick it up. But he'd never understand what I was trying
to say. "What?" he'd whisper. "You ate Nari's black pencil?"
So I'd have to whisper the whole thing to him or write him a
note, which were both dangerous propositions. So I'd give up
on trying to explain it and would just keep dropping my pencil
on the floor—having to enjoy this incommunicable treat alone.*

It was only a week or two later while I was running across the field to meet Ezra by the trees when Nari stopped me. "We know your little secret and find it very immature." She was wearing her Members Only jacket and she pulled her camera out from her pocket and took a picture of me.

"What secret?" I asked. I could think of a million secrets that I didn't want her to know. And I believed that she knew every one of them.

"Your language," she said. "It's very immature."

The language. Our precious useless language.

"Whatever." I ran for the pine trees as fast as I could.

I didn't understand what she meant. I didn't get how our language was immature. How else would you behave? At the time, I couldn't think of a single way to act more mature. A month later, she gave me a copy of the picture of my immature face. I had the look of someone watching an alien spaceship land.

When I told Ezra about the news, he said, "I know." And he wasn't banging his hand against the tree when he said, "I told Shayna after she let me kiss her."

"What?" I said. "We swore not to tell anyone. The language was ours!"

"Yeah," he said. "I know. But I just didn't see the point."

I didn't speak with him for two weeks. It's true that I did get over the loss of our whole silly language, and that we went back to being best friends, but it felt awfully important on that first night as my mom kept yelling for me to finally get out of the bathroom and start doing my homework. For Ezra, this language was a little game to play while he thought about a more satisfying way to behave. For me, this was all you could ask for: a broken way to communicate that was virtually unusable and still worth protecting at all costs.

Chapter Nine
Very Nearly Good News

Shmen steps into the restaurant, his smile exaggerated to cover up his limp. He sits down and asks, "How's it hanging?"

I ask him about the limp.

"You're supposed to say low and lazy," he tells me. "Or at least you might suggest a hang to the left. Unless you've got a center predilection, which suggests either a very small or very durable penis."

We order two burgers and two bourbons. This restaurant has mediocre food. The service is terrible. The place smells like rotten fries and the carpet is sticky from old beer. It takes forever to get your order, and consider yourself lucky if they get the order right. You walk out of here with a stomachache and smelling like beer-battered halibut—and they don't even serve fish. We both love coming here for lunch.

After telling him which way I'm hanging, he tells me about the limp. It turns out it's a new disease related to his old disease. The new disease is something that people often get a few years after being diagnosed with the old disease. At best, it means that he has something like rheumatoid arthritis. At worst, his joints and his spine will fuse together and his bones will eventually shatter.

"Enough about my diseases," he says. "Tell me about your diseases."

"What are you going to do about it?" I say.

He sips his bourbon and makes the sound of getting things out between his teeth. "They say physical therapy can help. The doc gave me some steroids which definitely help," he says. "Especially if I double the dose."

The scarier the story gets, the bigger he smiles.

"Does Julia know?" I ask. "Does Ally know?"

"Yes," he says. "She's worried," as if I just asked about one person. He sips on his empty glass.

"My novel very nearly has a plot," I tell him. "I've very nearly told Julia about the money I give you. I've very nearly stopped dreaming about my father. I've very nearly found a way to get out of my book deal. I've very nearly figured out how to live my life in my underwear while standing on my desk." I don't mention anything about Julia's thoughts of a baby because I've got nothing to very nearly say about it.

"It's very nearly good news," he says, and we toast to this nearly good news. But I can't keep my smile going for long. There's an image in my head of his spine fused together and I can't get rid of it.

After some silence and some staring at our empty glasses, Shmen says, "If you need more plot, why don't you have someone die? They say that death must come before rebirth anyhow."

"Who is they?" I ask.

#

We get our burgers and our second drinks and then a woman on her way out the door approaches Shmen.

"Joel?" she says. "I can't believe it. I was just thinking about you!" The woman is so tall and so skinny and so blonde and has such red lipstick on her lips that for a second I imagine that she's a cardboard figure of a woman. When Joel sees this woman he stands up and they hug and kiss two or three times and they express how nice it is to see each other and then they say bye but not before she makes Shmen promise to call her soon and then Shmen sits down as if nothing ever happened except that he sits down slowly because of his new disease and as he sits, I hear Shmen's grunt that is virtually unhearable.

"Do all six-foot-tall blondes do that to you?" I ask.

"That was Jessie," he says. "We worked at the university library together."

"Some library," I say.

He explains to me that last year he had a crush on her. That she had a crush on him. And I suggest that she still has a crush and he enjoys the accusation. And then I ask him what the hell a crush is anyway and he says it's when you get excited to see someone each day. It's when you send them too many e-mails and you fantasize about them, sometimes dream of having sex with them.

I don't say anything in response. I don't say anything for a good, long time.

"Crushes aren't bad," he says. "We didn't have sex or anything."

"But it's like cheating," I say. "Writing love letters and fantasizing about fucking like that. It's cheating," I say.

"No, it isn't," he says. "It's harmless. Pretty soon you forget about the crush anyhow. Maybe you can bring some of that crush energy into the relationship."

"The fuck you can," is what I say. And suddenly I can tell from Shmen's tightened forehead that I don't look so normal and so I try to breathe normally. I try to stop thinking about the napkin message.

"You should tell Julia," he says to me.

"What?" I say.

"You should tell Julia about the money." He finishes his drink. "And you should stop loaning me the money."

My face probably looks as overcooked as the burgers we both tried to finish.

"I should go," he says to me. "I've got to fail another interview." He gets himself out the chair. Then this man kisses me on the top of my head. "Take care of yourself, Yuval," he says. And then my brother-in-law leaves me at the table to pay for our tab. I notice that he not only limps on his way out, but that he can't turn his head without moving his chest too. Even his charming smile to the hostess is impeded.

It's been years since anyone has called me by my full Israeli name and it makes me feel like a child to hear it.

SO YOU DON'T WANT TO BE A JEW

There was a period when I rebelled against being Jewish. When I thought I could get out of the organization for good. I told my mom that I wasn't Jewish. That I thought the Torah was a big bunch of implausible shtuyot. I told her that I could never be a believer and I wanted to be a Buddhist. This is was what I told her on my first visit from college. With her pretty, Israeli accent, she said, "I can't believe you'd say this to me. What am I to do with this information? Mah la-asot?"

"Nothing," I told her. "I just wanted to be honest with you."

"What about your heritage?" she asked. "What about your culture?" She was nearly crying and I wished that I hadn't started the discussion. But once I started, it was tough to stop.

"I can still eat a Passover Seder," I said. "But you don't have to be Jewish to eat and drink like that."

My mother teared up and put her hand to her chest. "You're breaking my heart," she said.

"I'm sorry," I said to her, "but that's how I feel."

At the time, I thought this was the most mature way to communicate. This was my new understanding—to stick the knife inside, with no sense of timing or grace, and wiggle it.

It was then that I noticed my father hovering outside the living room.

When he walked in, he was shaking a finger at me like he had been giving this speech long before coming in to the room. "So you think you're no longer a Jew?" He spoke quietly—the voice he saved for when he was too angry to yell.

"Yes," I said, pretending to be confident.

"Well I've got news for you," he said. "If you're on an airplane and your plane gets hijacked and they get one look at your passport and see that your name is Yuval and that you were born in Israel, then I don't give two shits what you believe in. You'll be killed like a goddamn Jew."

No one said any more in that discussion. We each left the room and went to separate parts of the house. It's not that what he said sat perfectly right with me, but I never again tried to claim that I wasn't Jewish, no matter what I believed in.

Chapter Ten
Honey My Ass

So here is how it goes: Julia isn't home as usual. I'm at home
and restless as usual. The novel is going poorly as usual. But
unlike usual, she leaves her purse on the kitchen table. I don't
know how this can be, and for a second I think to worry
that something has happened to her, but then I come to the
conclusion that she must be fine because if anyone is going to
get in trouble, it will surely be me.

So I eat a roast beef sandwich beside her purse. Her purse
is black and has lots of compartments. I got it for her thirty-
three-and-one-third birthday, which she found strange. But
she loved the purse.

After the roast beef sandwich, I'm still hungry, but I
decide not to make another. And I keep staring at her purse.
I can't stop looking at it. And then I think about Save Me,
Julia. And I can't stop thinking about Save Me, Julia. And so
I try to leave the room. I try to pretend to write like usual but
all that appears on the page is Save Me Julia Save Me Julia
Save Me Julia Save Me Julia Save Me Julia Save Me Julia Save
Me Julia.

And so I go back to the purse and I do exactly what I
should not do.

Inside, just as expected, there are overflowing receipts
that she'll eventually throw away but can't bring herself to

toss quite yet. For the first time in our relationship, this habit annoys me. And so I keep pulling out receipts.

I get down on the kitchen floor and pour out her entire purse. It's a big mess of receipts and dollar bills. There's a wallet and a cell phone and some lipstick and eyeliner and a checkbook.

I spread everything out so no two items are on top of each other and it is then that I find a few crumbled napkins.

And on the napkins is that same crazy handwriting. Only this time, the phrases are even more obscure:

- Julia's Sexy Toes
- Julia and Her Babies
- Julia's Honor System Snack Box

I stare at these napkins, expecting to find the magic explanation to all my marital problems buried within these words. I look for a pattern. The S's are all so big and the J's are all so small. It must mean something. The man is surely a Jew hater. Julia's name is written quickly, as if this man is very familiar with her. And the phrase, Sexy Toes, is written all wiggly, like the man has just been sucking Julia's toes.

I could make up a million stories about these napkins. But I'd have confidence in none.

#

I first notice Julia's black pumps right there on the floor. And then her stockings. And her dress. And there she is. Standing above me, watching me rummage through her purse.

"Honey," I say. "You're home."

"Honey my ass," she says. And she has a point.

Chapter Eleven
Alcohol and Steroids

I'm not saying that you would get yourself into this mess. But even so, what would you do in this situation? You could respond by getting angry at your tall, gentile wife. You could accuse her of sleeping with other men: "You whore!" you could announce. Or you could respond to her by apologizing for invading her privacy: "I'm so sorry for going through your purse. I'm ashamed of myself." Or you could mix these two responses. You could say: "I shouldn't have been going through your purse but what the hell are these napkins about?" Or you could dodge the whole issue and get to something deeper: tell her that you want to have a baby.

All these responses seem reasonable. But I choose none of them. I use a different kind of response, which involves curling your body around your beautiful wife's legs and saying directly to her black pumps, "I didn't do it."

She takes in a deep breath. I can hear it all the way down on the cold floor. Then she shakes me off her foot and leaves the room.

#

I do eventually get up, and I do eventually find my wife in the bedroom. It's our bedroom, but at the moment, it feels like hers. She is sitting on the side of the bed and I sit next to her and she lets me.

I'm holding the napkins in my hand even though I don't remember picking them up. I sort them in alphabetical order because I don't know how to begin, and Julia is staring at the wall, doing a good job of not helping me out. She is angry. I can tell by how stiffly she sits. But she is still giving me an opportunity to say something. An opportunity that I hardly deserve or know what to do with.

Maybe she doesn't want me to talk. Maybe she's ashamed about whatever she is involved in. It's all too much to think about. Her napkin-based affair.

"I'm worried about Shmendrik," I tell her. "He isn't looking so good." I put my hand on Julia's lap. "He can't beat this thing with just alcohol and steroids."

My wife puts her head against my shoulder. Slowly, piece by piece, her body begins to slump, and she cries. And then it's not just crying. It's wailing. And I realize that I've never witnessed her cry for more than a fraction of a second. Usually, when she cries, she walks away fast, goes into the bathroom, flushes the toilet once or twice, and comes out asking me about lunch or overdue library books. Protestants have this uncanny ability to flush their problems in one toilet visit. Even the baggage she carries about her mother stays in the bathroom most of the time. But now Julia cries like it's all she knows how to do. And I squeeze her into my shoulder and chest. We've never been in this situation. And so I keep squeezing her. I rub her back. I let this woman cry.

HOW I KILLED HER MOTHER

It finally happened. Her mother finally left her father. There was no question that it was necessary. What took Julia until fifteen to realize (and run away from) took her mother until fifty-nine.

Her mother was beautiful—the way her gray hair rolled past her shoulders like some kind of rainstorm and the way her cheeks swelled from a laughter that could have been from a joke either minutes or decades passed. But there was little laughter for this woman who left a man after spending so many years of her life serving his needs. After you cut off a problem limb, what do you use to replace it? For her mother, it turns out that it required a flask full of Monopolowa—potato-based and only $16 a liter.

Julia had just bought a new house. Two-car garage. Three bedrooms. And she was single again. Loads of space. Why not invite her mother to live with her? They loved each other. They watched Marlon Brando films together. They ordered Picasso and Van Gogh prints. They danced to Frank Sinatra together. They bought season passes to the museum and to the symphony. They could share the gas bill and complain together about the neighbor's pro-Republican front-yard signage.

But it turns out vodka couldn't completely fill her mother's missing limb. It took Julia herself to fill the hole. And why shouldn't Julia help? It was a chance for them to get reacquainted as two adults.

Her mother could dance the way a weeping willow sways in a breeze. And she was great about listening to Julia complain about working too many hours as a marketing manager at whatever corporation she was working at. Julia could even tell such unmeaningful stories like how her coworker Joseph started sleeping with her other coworker Joseph. Her mother would listen.

As a loyal daughter, Julia kept away from dating men for a year, made sure her mother had settled into her new life. That kind of change isn't easy. But it's not easy to be single and taking care of Mama when you're thirty either.

After the first date that Julia went out on, she thought her mother's worry was a normal concern. After all, the man had sent a suspiciously large bouquet of flowers the day before and who knows what that could have meant. And so it seemed okay that her mother drank a little too much that night and that she was in tears when Julia came home.

But every time Julia went out, she had to confront another panic, even over men who were tediously unthreatening. Julia's brother could go out with drug addicts and her mother didn't care, but for Julia, even a librarian was dangerous material. Her relationships fell apart before they could start. But after all, she did love her mother more than these men of questionable intentions. And so she accepted this predicament. That she'd have to calm her mother frequently, that sometimes she'd have to chase her mother down the street, that sometimes she'd have to hear her mother call her a whore. Her poor mother, she thought. All those years with a man who read the TV Guide more than he spoke with his wife.

When we met, she had already learned to preface the first date with a warning about her baggage: "It's like I'm carrying around the Empire State Building in my purse." But baggage or no baggage, a girl who could so easily outwit me, who could practically tolerate my neuroses, who could sneak a hand on my lap while telling me about Brando and Sinatra was a woman that I wanted to stick with. That night I was completely unconcerned about her 365,000-ton purse.

We learned to work around the issues. We saw each other when we could. But our trysts were short and they ended abruptly; we had to sneak around like fifteen-year-olds. Within six months, it began to bother me. I was dying for her to spend the night at my place. I was dying for us to take a trip together. I grew to resent her beautiful damn mother, who called every time I got even one finger in Julia's pants.

Julia realized that something had to change. Maybe she wanted more than one finger in her pants. I had plenty other fingers to spare. So she told her mother, "You need to let me have my own life." Her mother couldn't say no to something this reasonable, so she said, "Yes," even though inside her chest, she was yelling NO in languages that she had never spoken before. I know this feeling.

Julia and I finally got our time alone together, though Julia noticed the signs of her mother's collapse. She saw the poorly cleaned vomit stains on her mother's bedroom floor. She smelled the fermentation on her mother's skin. She noticed the way her mother had trouble remembering the things that seemed unforgettable.

Julia has not once blamed me for anything that happened to her mother, even though I feel this burden any time that Julia gets sad. That perhaps it was me that killed her mother. Because it was me that convinced Julia that it was okay for the two of us to go to Oaxaca. It was me who convinced Julia at the airport that she didn't need to worry about the unlocked cabinet with the vodka in it. I remember it clearly, how I took Julia in my arms and said with an insincere sort of confidence, "Honey, it'll be fine. Your mother can take care of herself," and, for that blissful week in Mexico, we left all 365,000 tons behind.

Chapter Twelve
The Whole Megillah

Julia has basically cried into all the napkins before either of us remembers how this whole thing got started. She tells me about how she's so worried about her brother and how he's so stubborn about his health and how she's scared to bug him any more about it. And I agree with her, because I agree with her. And after she has ruined the unfaithful napkins with her tears and snot, I take them out of her hands and put them in my pocket.

"Julia," I say to my wife. "I need to talk to you."

Her crying slows. And then it's just funny breathing. And then I begin talking. "I've been giving Shmen money every month for his debts," I say. "I've been pulling money out of what's left of my parents' inheritance without telling you. I've been cutting myself again."

I can't gauge Julia's reaction because she's still sniffling and I'm not sure if she's upset about Shmen's health or if it's now about the money or about me or us or the purse or the napkins or the fact that I don't like BLTs no matter how many times she makes them. I've lost track of the emotional steps and now I'm terrified of saying anything. This is why I once asked my wife if we could conduct our relationship through letters only. In person, there is too much to interpret and worry about.

But she does eventually look up at me and what I see isn't the friendliest face in the world. "Since you've been going through my purse," she says. "Did you notice anything addressed to you?"

"You mean like a napkin?" I say.

"No. I mean like a check."

I leave my weepy wife at the bed and run into the kitchen. I know exactly where I placed that check on the kitchen floor. I even remember acknowledging—in some foggy part of my brain—that it was addressed to me. So I grab the check and come back into the room. The check from Shmen is big enough that I assume it covers all that he owes me.

And, in a way, I'm disappointed. Just like that—*poof*—my horrible beautiful insane secret has disappeared.

"Have you known for a while?" I ask.

She doesn't say anything. She stares at the wall as seriously as Orthodox Jews stare at the Wailing Wall when they pray. Except my wife and I aren't the praying type. So I assume that she's waiting for me to ask the real question. When they pray to that wall in Jerusalem, Jews sometimes put little crumbled pieces of paper inside the cracks. These have their hopes and wishes and dreams on them. I often wonder what kind of message I would put inside this wall, if I were the praying type. But I keep coming up blank. And so I pull the crumbled napkins out of my pocket and hand them to Julia.

"Who are you *shtuping*?" I ask.

She points to one of the restraints, which is still hanging from the bedpost. "Pretty much no one," she says.

My gentile wife is more familiar with my culture than I give her credit for. She understands the nuance of the Yiddish language. For instance, she understands that spanking your husband is not technically *shtuping*. It falls more in the realm of *meshuganah*.

"Then who is writing these notes?" I ask.

"You don't recognize the handwriting?" She gives them back to me.

I try to open one up and look at it but the ink is smudged and wet. "No."

"Well then look at that check," she says.

And that's when it hits me. Shmen and his obsession with obscure band names. He can spend hours Googling for band names—that's how he got fired from his last job. My wife is looking at me. I know she's wondering how it's possible an idiot like me could've scored a 1390 on the GRE. And so I try to think of something to say. I try to come up with some way to explain why I've been brooding for months about money and napkin dilemmas that don't even exist. I need to give my wife an eloquent explanation for my madness.

And so I say, "Oh."

"Jesus, Yuvi!" she says. She gets up fast. "This is how you live your life?" Julia grabs my pants and pulls them down enough to see the cuts on my ass. Then she lifts them back up. "No wonder you have no plot in your novel! You get fixated on the smallest things and can't move forward."

I know I deserve this, and so I sit down on the bed and take it. Julia is pacing the bedroom. I'm expecting a big, long speech and I'm preparing to apologize. But instead of it going the way I expect and prepare for, she suddenly slows down. She walks up to me. My body tightens up and I squint, preparing for the explosion, hoping that if I wish hard enough, I might disappear. I'd even be willing to pray for it to work out.

And then Julia leans over me and she kisses me on the top of my head. "I sure do love you," she says to me.

And that's when I know that things are far worse than I ever suspected.

THE SMALLEST THINGS

The age: eight years old. For both Ezra and me. And for Adam Silver, whose birthday party it was. The setting: Adam Silver's house. Adam's father, dressed as a bad clown (with a sweet smell coming off his skin that I'd later connect to alcoholics), had just finished his performance and we were all sitting on the living room floor playing with the twisted balloon objects he had given us. He claimed that they were elephants and giraffes and houses but they were just tangled messes. Even so, his excitement while naming these tangled creatures gave us the authority to twist them up further and call them whatever we wanted: a racing car, a naked girl hanging from the jungle gym, Tyrannosaurus rex. We were loving it.

By we, I mean all the kids but one. The one not playing was Ezra, who had recently crawled over to the corner of the room and sat there quietly, hoping to disappear. Ezra had pissed in his pants so badly that his jeans were wet down to his knees.

But I didn't see him in the corner. I was too wrapped up in the sound of twisting the narrow balloons around each other, and how amazing it was that they seemed unpoppable. There were boys at the party, there were girls at the party, but I actually don't remember a single face or name. All I remember is Ezra Roth in the corner, whom I wasn't even watching at the time.

Until I heard Adam Silver yell, "Hey! Look! Ezra peed in his pants!" Adam yelled this out even though he knew that Ezra had gotten him Mousetrap for his birthday, as he'd asked. And just like that, all ten of us jumped Ezra Roth.

Imagine this: (1) My best friend red-faced and ashamed, completely silent, sitting in the corner with his knees in the air higher than his slouchy body. (2) Nine children trying to spread Ezra's legs, boys and girls laughing and making fun of how wet he was. "What a baby!" they yelled. (3) And then me, one little boy, crying and trying to squeeze Ezra's legs together, whining, "Stop it! Stop it! Stop it!" like the act of closing his legs could make this whole unpleasant scene disappear.

Throughout all this craziness, Ezra didn't say a word; he just let his legs open and close like they weren't part of his body. Eventually, Adam's mother ran into the room and broke up the party. She took Ezra with her while Adam's dad tried to distract us—he did an impeccable imitation of John Belushi as a king bee from Saturday Night Live, which none of us understood. A few minutes later Ezra walked out of the bathroom with a pair of Adam's sweatpants—Adam's favorite pair, apparently.

I wouldn't explain to my mother why I was crying so badly when she picked me up. When we got home, she had to call Adam's mother to get the story. And then my mother looked at me, all confused, as if she wished I had wet my pants as well, so as to explain my hysteria.

The next day, nobody said anything, not a word about this whole event. Even Ezra acted like nothing had happened. And so I kept my mouth shut. But I cried that next night as well. When my mom came into my bedroom, I told her that I had a cold, and so she gave me some chewable Tylenol, a remedy she used for many of my bouts of angst.

Ezra would later become a highly acclaimed surgeon. He'd be famous for his success in performing high-risk operations on children. I've been toying with calling him one of these days. It's a little tricky to know how to phrase something like, "Remember that time when you pissed in your pants and I was trying to force your crotch closed? Because I think about that all the time!"

It's not that I'm scared to call him. I don't call him because I know what he'll say: "I guess I just don't remember that." It's not because he has blocked out the event. It's not because he is in denial or has some part of him that is stuck in his childhood. It's not a deficiency. He doesn't remember because it wasn't a memorable event for him. It was one of a thousand blips along the road of his childhood. Ezra Roth is a man who has to go up to a young couple in the waiting room and say to them that he has just seen their five-year-old son die on the operating table. And then he has to go back into the operating room and do it all over again with another child. Ezra Roth can't afford to dwell on how he pissed his pants in 1980.

I don't have to do the things in a day's work that Ezra has to do. Some days, I don't interact with a single person. But I do often think about Ezra Roth. And sometimes I even think about Adam Silver's dad in those days when he looked so happy. And I imagine the sound of balloons squeaking when twisted into absurd shapes, expecting them to pop.

Chapter Thirteen
Family

A few weeks into living with the knowledge that napkin men don't exist, I catch Julia moping on the couch.

It's a rare sight to actually catch Julia feeling down. For Julia, feeling down causes her to move faster, to do more, to be more than her already-complete self, to save twenty families rather than just ten. Down keeps her up on her feet. As for me, down is down. So when I see her in the living room lying on the couch, staring at the ceiling, looking nearly as helpless as me, I'm pretty damn scared.

"Julia," I say. "What happened?" I expect her to tell me a story of how one of her alcoholics has died, so it scares me even more when she reaches out for my hand and pulls me toward her. Her hand is warm and sweet and soft and I don't know what to do with it.

She says to me in a quiet and scratchy voice, "When my mom would try to get Joel and me to bed, she'd do this thing where she'd have us hide under the sheets. She'd leave the room for a few seconds, and then she'd run in and tickle us through the sheets."

I put my hand in Julia's hair and scratch her head. "It sounds awfully scary," I say.

"It's one of the happiest moments I can remember."

It takes an adjustment in my mind to make this scene happy. I have to make the sounds and colors and smells a little bit different.

I have to change the mood of the characters. I have to think of Joel and Julia so pleased to be hiding together. I have to put that gorgeous giggle on Julia's face. And suddenly, I can picture the scene just as sentimental and beautiful as she meant it.

"I want a family," Julia says to me. "I want to have a family."

I stop scratching her head.

There's the fact that we haven't had anything that approaches baby-making sex in years. There's the fact that our communication is nearly as tangled and broken as Shmen's large intestine when the surgeons pulled it out of his body. There's the fact that Julia didn't exactly say that she wants a family *with me*, she just wants a family. I might not be in the picture at all. And there's the fact that I feel a terror somewhere deep in my chest when thinking about being responsible for another thing that breathes.

I could ask her to expand on what she wants. I could discuss this subject further. I could explain my various thoughts about family—some positive and some terrified. But what I do is something more self-involved and more cowardly, something less sincere and less open to discussion.

I say, "I don't want a fucking kid because I'll be an asshole like my dad." And then I walk out of the room. I walk out of the house and don't come back for hours.

This is how my dad dealt with complicated subjects when I was a kid. Except when he walked out of the room, I always pictured that he had an unwavering feeling about the matter, that he was convinced of being right.

But I now understand that my father walked away from discussions with the exact feeling I get after walking away— an instant sense of regret, confident that I've dealt with the situation poorly, and wondering why the hell I always fuck everything up for no good reason.

LAYING EGGS

My father did this thing with children where he pretended he could lay eggs. After the first time he did it to me, I asked him to do it again and again. And he did this trick for years and years. I best remember when he did it to my little cousin, David. At the time I was maybe sixteen or eighteen and David was maybe six or eight. It was at my aunt and uncle's place after dinner; we were celebrating someone's birthday or mourning someone's death or celebrating some Jewish holiday or perhaps atoning for our many sins.

My father came out of the kitchen and sat with David on the living room couch. "You know," my father whispered. "I can lay eggs."

David thought about this for a moment and then said, "Nuh-uh!"

"It's true. I could lay one for you right now."

"Only birds lay eggs," David said. A boy who had clearly read a book or two about who lays eggs and who doesn't. "Mommies make babies a different way. Eggs aren't the way."

"Now, normally I'd agree with you," my dad said, "but I can sit here right next to you and lay an egg on this couch. I could make you an omelet with my eggs."

"Show me," David said, still skeptical.

My father scrunched his face tight. He opened his mouth and groaned loud enough for people in the kitchen to come into the living room to see what was going on. And then my father stood up.

"He did it!" David said, and he stood up off the couch and pointed and yelled. "He did it he did it he did it he did it!" David

grabbed the egg and ran around the house showing everybody what my father had just given birth to.

We left the party soon after that, with David in the corner of the living room grunting, trying his best to lay an egg.

About two hours later, we got the call. My mother picked up the phone and listened to my uncle's situation. "You need to get your tuches back there. David has already made kahkee into two pairs of pajamas."

My father drove those fifteen miles for the second time in order to reveal his trick, which David would end up using on his own children twenty years later.

And that's one of the things I loved about my dad. He had a charm that was powerful enough to cause you to shit your pants twice in one night, trying to lay a damn egg.

Chapter Fourteen
Shmuvi

"Dude, I need a favor." It's a reflex of mine to look for my checkbook when Shmen calls. But then he says, "I'm supposed to pick Maddy up from school today, except that my knee isn't behaving."

And as I try to formulate a question about the behavior of his knee, he says, "Someone needs to be at her school in twenty-five minutes."

#

Ally has told me it's a ritual that her daughter loves. She runs out of the school giggling whenever Shmen picks her up.

I don't even know if she'll recognize me. I've only met her a few times. But when I step into the school and look around the after-care area, this cute little blonde-haired girl runs up and hugs me. She squeezes me tightly and I'm tempted to explain to this girl all the reasons that I'm not such a huggable person: I'm a coward. I worry all the time. I'm a poor communicator. I can't stop thinking about my dead father, even while my wife is trying to seduce me. I obsess over napkins. I can't please my wife. I'm a narcissist.

But when Maddy stops hugging, I'm tempted to ask her to do it again.

"I guess you know who I am," I say.

"Of course!" She holds my hand and begins to drag me out of the school. "You're Joelly's brother!"

#

Maddy is carrying a book with her called *The Gorilla Did It*. When I ask her about it, she says it's great because it's about a gorilla that wakes up a sleeping boy and convinces him to mess up his room. When the boy gets in trouble, he explains to his mother that the gorilla did it.

I start to wonder how I might use this phrase. For instance, if I'm standing on my desk in my underwear and my wife comes in, pissed off that I didn't pick up the groceries like I promised, I could say, "It's not me, the gorilla did it." And when my wife puts her hand down my pants and feels that soft and scared little organ, I could say, "The gorilla did it!" When my editor asks for the novel, I'll tell her, "The gorilla took it."

It would solve a lot of problems.

On the drive home, Maddy tells me story after story about her day as if I were a part of her family and it makes me feel so glad to be around her. She tells me the rules of Everybody's It Tag and she explains how boys smell more like dirt and how girls smell more like flowers and she tells me that her teacher's father died last week and she tells me that her best friend has four cats, three ferrets, and twenty-seven tomatoes. And then she asks me how to spell Poop Mobile.

"Poop Mobile?" I ask. "What's that?"

"It's the truck that picks you up when you have to poop so bad that you need to go to the hospital."

"Does Joelly ever go to the hospital?" I ask, trying to sound casual even while I'm scared to hear the answer.

"Not really," she says. "And did you know that the Poop Mobile is made out of bulletproof glass?"

"Well that makes sense," I say.

"And did you know," she tells me, "you can't spell husband without anus?"

Maddy pretty much controls the conversation the whole car ride home. She's under ten and she's more confident than the me that my therapist makes me write about when I'm trying to pretend I'm overconfident.

"I have a crush on a boy," she says.

"You do? Already?"

"What do you mean already? He is my fourth, if you count David."

"Let's count him," I say.

"Me and Jeffrey are going to buy a four-bedroom house. We'll need three cars so that we can always have one for our friends. And we want three kids—two girls. We're going to Hawaii for our honeymoon."

"Wow," I say. "You've got more plans than I've ever had."

I glance her way and see that she is pondering this observation. That she has it more together than a so-called adult. "Where did you go," she says, "on your honeymoon with Aunt Julia?"

"Oh," I say. "We went to cremate my father in North Carolina." It comes out without me thinking about it. I see Maddy try to parse my answer. But, fortunately, not try too hard.

"Does North Carolina have a beach?" she says.

"Better you should tell me more about you and Jeffrey," I say, scared of what I might tell her next.

As I'm sitting there enjoying her breathlessly told stories, she asks me if Aunt Julia is still mad at me.

"Mad about what?" And then I realize I'm using a seven-year-old to get to the crux of my relationship issues.

"You know," she says. "About your problems."

"Which ones?"

#

I take a few wrong turns, which suits Maddy just fine. I could take a 2,500-mile wrong turn and she'd have plenty to talk about.

"Tell me about when you and Joelly were kids," she says.

I think about explaining to her how I didn't grow up with Joel. That we're not related. I think about explaining the difference between blood relatives and in-laws.

And then I say, "You know Hawaii is actually made up of seven different islands."

#

When I finally drop Maddy off at her mother's barn, Ally gives me a big hug. It's a more adult version of Maddy's hug but just as comforting. We agree that the four of us should go out again. And then Ally says something else: "You should come back here soon. Just you. When you have time. I want to show you my horses."

Ally isn't a tall woman. She is probably five feet tall in regular life. But standing beside her barn, as she points to it, as she wears those big boots, as she gives me a half smile, she seems a foot taller than me. Her hair is messy from whatever it is she does in her barn.

It feels like she's coming on to me. A secret. In a barn. Just me, her, and the horses. How can that not be wrong? But I know that I'm misunderstanding something. Sometimes I just feel too dumb to understand this world.

When I was a kid, my dad kept a jar sitting on the bookshelf that said "Great Truths" on it. When I asked him what that meant, he said it was a joke, because no truth is greater than another. For years, I walked around our house wondering what was so funny about that.

"Yes, I'd like that," I say to Ally, "but right now I've got to meet Julia."

Which is a "Great Lie."

My dad kept nothing but paperclips inside that jar of truths. I wonder what Ally keeps inside that barn of hers. But I still leave. I leave faster than you can say *Oy veyshmir*.

But as I'm running away from Ally and her barn, I still manage to hear a nice goodbye from Maddy. She says, "See you later, Shmuvi!" And she says it like Shmuvi has always been my name.

THE GORILLA DID IT

My brother Joelly was five years old when he realized you could use a black permanent marker to draw all over every piece of furniture in your parents' house. I was eight at the time, old enough to know that when my dad got home, my brother would be in sincerely deep shit.

I tend to think the world is a dangerous place to be. Even when things are going well, I'm trying to anticipate how soon I will get screwed. This holds true for my jobs, my relationships, my friendships, my finances, my family. I feel helpless against the world and am always expecting that meteor to crash onto my house. When an ex-girlfriend told me she had been lying to me for months and sleeping with another man—a bigger, stronger, richer, more handsome man—I wasn't angry or offended. I accepted this fact gracefully. Because that is how the world works. In that same conversation, I even thanked her for not being more cruel.

But my brother saw things differently. He saw the world as something amusing, something that could be played with. Even when dealing with my father—a man who could get so angry you'd have to steer clear of him for days at a time—my brother looked for ways to make the relationship interesting. He could be in control of a situation, even at five.

Earlier that day, my mother had read to us. After reading this book, my mother began cooking dinner, I began playing with my Legos, and my brother began drawing all over every piece of furniture in the house.

A nasty aspect of my being scared of the world is that I sometimes want those who live so casually and comfortably to be punished. And when I saw what my brother had done and that gorgeous smile of his, black marks all over his face and shirt, I stepped away and savored the notion he would have to pay for this joy.

When my father came home, he went straight to his office to drop off his briefcase. I heard him yell out, "What in the hell happened here?"

My father ran into my room with the marker he found on the floor. "Did you do this?" he yelled. You could see the veins going through his temples. He shook the marker in his hand and then threw it on the floor.

"No," I said. "I promise." And I prayed for him to leave my room.

He then ran into my brother's room.

"Who did this?" I heard him yell. And I suddenly regretted all my evil thoughts about wanting my brother to pay for his sins. It was terrible to think of my brother receiving my father's wrath alone. So I ran into my brother's room as well, thinking he could use my help. I didn't have my brother's wit, but I was another body to stand in the way.

My brother's face and shirt were all marked up. And he held out his ink-stained hands, as if this gesture were proving his innocence, instead of sealing his fate. My father's hands were tight in fists. My mother had already run into the room, and we both were too scared to say a thing, for fear of causing those fists to move.

And that's when my little brother said with utter confidence, "The gorilla did it."

It was unfathomable that my father would let go of what had just been done to his furniture. But my father's next words were, "Where the hell is this gorilla?" And he yelled it like he was going to beat the hell out of this animal when he found him.

"You just missed him," my brother explained, and he pointed at the window.

"Well, he better watch himself," my father said. And he left room while trying to hold in his smile.

Chapter Fifteen
Everyone Loves Me

It should be easier these days. My wife isn't sleeping with napkin men. In fact, she even wants to have kids with me. I apologized for walking out in the middle of our last discussion. I told her I needed some time to think about it and she said that was okay. I told her, again, that I would stop cutting myself, again, and she was okay with this promise, again. Even my novel is going okay. I have fifteen chapters written so far. But I know better than to think I can sit pretty. Something ugly is coming on. So I spend a lot of time pacing around my house while Julia is away, which is a lot of the time.

Under the mattress, I have a picture of Julia when she was two years old. It was her birthday. She is wearing a paper hat that says "Everyone Loves Me" on the front. Julia is in her mother's arms and she has a giggle on her face that is impossible not to smile at. I don't need to hide this picture, but I do. I want it all to myself.

Now that she's proven to me that napkins aren't malignant and that she wants to have a family, I feel even less confident about our relationship. It's even more unlikely for us to have normal sex. I'm even more obsessed that she is sick of me, wants me to be different than the me that I am. And she sighs too often. And our teasing seems more out of resentment than out of love.

I've never been to Florida or Louisiana or the Caribbean during a storm but I have this fictionalized image of what it's like to be in the eye of the hurricane from watching too many disaster movies. And that's what the quiet of my day feels like. Like a movie version of the eye of a hurricane. And when my beautiful wife who loves me and wants to have children steps into my office at a time when she should be busy with her job, I know she is the ugly hurricane that is all around me.

There is nothing ugly about Julia. Maybe this is part of the problem. I'm too nervous to pee standing up and she can arrange a meeting with the governor. I go to the therapist and she wins a salsa dancing contest. I want to be spanked and she wants a family.

My wife doesn't stutter. She isn't slow to speak. But her voice is so soft that it is hard to tell where in the room the words are coming from. "Honey," she says. "I need some time off."

"Well, then get off your feet," I say. "Let me give you a massage." For however soft and thoughtful her voice is, mine is loud and dumb-sounding. But I stand up. I'm ready. I'm ready to do whatever it is I need to do.

"It's too late," she says. She is too calm.

"No," I say. "I'll even put on a new pair of underwear. It's only ten in the morning. I could give you a nine-hour massage before sunset. What's hurting? Your inguinal ligaments? I just read a special technique for inguinal ligaments."

"Honey," she says. "I'm serious."

"I am too," I say. "Tell me what you need and I'll do it."

The fair skin around her eyes makes the red more noticeable, and I see that she doesn't look great today, and I see she is tired, and I realize she's been tired for more than just today, and I realize it's more than just because of a busy week.

My wife, she looks around my office, a room that reeks of insecurity. "I don't need anything," she says. "Or at least nothing here."

"I learned a new recipe for BLTs," I say. "It involves putting the L before the B and the T. Technically it's an LBT, but I think you'll still like it. The Protestant Sandwich Committee gives it five stars."

I can feel myself drowning. I'm grabbing for anything I can get ahold of. I'm trying to stay afloat. But it's too late. All these stupid jokes when I should be saying: Please don't leave. I love you. Let's talk about it. Give me another chance.

"Honey," she says in a tone as warm and kind as you could ever ask for. "I rented an apartment."

And that's when it hits me: not even a Protestant sandwich can save me now.

#

As Julia packs her things, she sings "Raindrops Keep Falling on My Head." Even though she is crying and she can barely speak, this song continues for what seems like forever. So I lock myself in the bathroom and cover my ears.

And I'd sooner tell you a story about Uranus than tell you more about the way Julia leaves me.

Book 3
URANUS

MEN ARE FROM MARS, JULEFS ARE FROM URANUS

Stories never take place on Uranus. But this one does. And it does so without a lick of mockery for the planet's name, which typically finds itself in as many joke books as scientific journals.

The hero of our story arrives on Uranus for one simple reason: to save our solar system. Our hero is so famous that even an alien stationed on Uranus wants to meet him. In real life, our hero is a nobody who sits around in his torn underwear, trying to write a novel about a man trying to write a novel. But instead, he ends up writing silly stories about Uranus. In real life, this man is timid and scared. He weeps at night. He has problems communicating. In real life, our hero is impotent when it relates to the bedroom and his wife. But in this science fiction story, our hero is blond and bold and beautiful. He is virile. He is a brilliant tactician, and he is the last hope for mankind. Our hero is the most famous political advisor on Earth, and now he has one hour to negotiate with a JuLef alien creature who is tasked with blowing up our solar system. This creature is the last of his species.

It is worth mentioning that JuLefs look to us like monkeys. This is by design. It was the 1959 flight when we launched Able and Baker, a rhesus monkey and a squirrel monkey respectively, into space that the JuLefs first noticed our solar system and our cute little space program. So the JuLefs sent their first fleet of negotiators in the form of rhesus monkeys. As far as we could tell, they were identical to monkeys, arriving even with fleas in their hair. We would never have been able to distinguish them from our own monkeys—except they could talk.

#

At first, the JuLefs inhabited Uranus. Thousands of them. And they waited. They waited for our knowledge to progress to a point that merited communication. But after two hundred years, they grew impatient with our slow progress. "They should have kept the monkeys in charge of the space program," the JuLef negotiators agreed. And so they decided to visit the crude Mars outpost we had recently built.

The story goes this way: we first met them on Mars; we last met them on Uranus. On Mars, it was charming. We were curious, awestruck. It was incredible. Intelligent life! Brilliant monkeys who traveled by thought, manipulated time by choice, and ate entire stars for lunch. They shared their knowledge with us, and we shared our classic films with them. For us, this meant mental-powered flight. For them, it meant Marlon Brando in On the Waterfront. *It was a grand time. The most saladacious of all our species' salad days!*

But on Uranus, the party was over. They saw us for what we were. Insecure, afraid of exposing our weaknesses, jealous and angry and destructive. We always wanted more than what we had and we would destroy ourselves to get it. To think that we would try to hijack the JuLef/Earth project when these creatures could see through space and time! It was either stupid or a death wish. Let's say both.

On Mars, we were intriguing and cute: funny creatures with that funny little digestive system and that way we liked to hump each other for amusement. But on Uranus, our species had been deemed unworthy troublemakers, doomed to sit in time-out for an eternity. It would take one JuLef thought to destroy the sun. There goes the neighborhood. And it was up to our hero to convince this last JuLef negotiator that we were worth saving.

In real life, this meeting didn't take place on Uranus, it happened at the Urban Grind coffee shop on 22nd and Irving. In real life, he wasn't trying to save all of humanity, he was just trying to save his measly little marriage. In real life, he wasn't equipped with a neutron bomb. This man couldn't even sustain an erection.

#

Uranus is composed of gas and ice. Surface temperature—if you can call it a surface—is negative 360 degrees Fahrenheit. Even with our newfound skill at M.P.F., it would have taken 10.5 years to make the trip. And it would have required the latest technology in thermal underwear. But this JuLef made it happen in a warm seven seconds, which is even faster than the speed of light. In the early days of our relationship, the JuLefs respected our laws of physics. But the honeymoon was over.

Our hero steps out of the spaceship and steps into what looks like an Earth coffee shop. Except instead of soothing café music, there is a screeching sound from the speakers. This screeching causes our hero to forget the tune he was humming in the spaceship, a tune he wanted to remember.

The JuLef negotiator is the only one in the place and he is sitting at a table waiting for our hero. This is the first and only time the JuLefs have made us visit them on Uranus. They used to come to us. Or meet us at a Mars café. In either case, they stayed politely in our neighborhood. But after the little incident—our failed coup—they no longer were interested in our convenience.

Our hero covers his ears as he sits down next to the monkey-shaped JuLef negotiator. The monkey snaps his monkey fingers and the noise stops.

"Your species' auditory sense was always a tricky one for us," the monkey admits.

Our hero looks around at the place. It reminds him of a coffee shop from back home, but he can't quite place it. The café has the strange quality of feeling recently inhabited, but also it feels like it has been permanently abandoned. The cappuccino on the front counter is still steaming.

"Nice work on the café," our hero says.

The monkey points all around but doesn't explain what he's pointing at. He picks at some fleas and then eats them. "They've strapped a neutron bomb to your genitals."

Our hero adjusts his pants—the device is incredibly small, but he now realizes he wore the wrong underwear for the occasion. He points over to the cappuccino he's been staring at. "That is exactly what I want," he says. One flaw with the Earthlings' plan to blow up this JuLef with a neutron bomb is that our hero has about as much interest in saving mankind as does this JuLef.

"Oh yes," the monkey says. "The cappuccino is for you."

On the way to the counter, our hero is surprised at how unfrightened he is by this meeting. But it's not courage as much as apathy. In his time, our hero has advised four presidents, three chancellors, two planetary rulers, and one extremely controversial urologist. His résumé is brilliant but his heart is cold. Since he saw his father leave his mother alone with three kids and absolutely nothing other than a collection of useless stamps from our ancient First Civil War, our hero has been skeptical of the heart. It has left him as cold as the gases of Uranus.

So now our hero walks over to get his cappuccino, which he has been dreaming about for hours, for days—it seems like for his whole life. At the counter, along with the cappuccino, he finds a Lamy pen, which he decides to pick up, the monkey won't be needing it anyhow, and then he comes back to sit with his monkey friend. But as he walks back, he notices one tile on the floor is missing. The hole in the floor goes straight through to the gaseous mass of Uranus. He takes the pen and drops it down the hole. It disappears without a sound.

"Stay clear of the hole," the monkey says without looking back. For a minute, our hero thinks of jumping in.

Our real-life hero dreams of having such a detached coldness. But in real life, when our hero's wife arrives at the coffee shop, our hero says, "I missed you so much," because she left the house a month prior. She left him because she got tired of him, because who wouldn't get tired of a man in his underwear who does nothing other than fail to write a novel? In real life, after the hero's wife gives our hero a good, long stare, she sits down next to him and says, "You weren't supposed to contact me."

But our sci-fi hero doesn't long for or beg from anyone. He sits down at that table, next to a flea-eating alien, and sips on his triple-shot cappuccino as if it is the only thing in the solar system that he wants.

"Did you know," the monkey says, "that Brando improvised that scene with Eva Marie Saint?"

"What?" our hero says.

"On the Waterfront," the JuLef says, disappointed again with our species. "The scene where he picks up her glove and tries it on. That was Brando's improvised work."

"Ahh," our hero says, more interested in the coffee than a two-hundred-year-old movie.

"Do you know why I wanted to see you?" the JuLef says.

Our hero keeps sipping his cappuccino. He looks up at the monkey and wonders how much longer he has left to enjoy this drink.

"It's because you just don't care," the monkey says. "You are unusual to your species in this way. You don't care to save your people, your planet, or yourself. In twenty minutes, I will think your solar system into smithereens and you don't give the ass of a rat."

Our hero's stomach starts grumbling in a crampy way and he knows he'll have to go to the bathroom soon. Maybe it's good, he decides, that he'll be blown up before he has to confront this potentially troubling bowel movement.

"But since you are not driven by fear or longing," the monkey continues, "you also have the freedom to choose what you want in any situation."

"If you can see through time and space," our hero says, "then why did you bother with us?" The cappuccino is strong, a little too strong, and he can already feel the agitation. "I don't trust my species and I'm one of them."

"We saw this coming," the JuLef says. "But we still got what we wanted." He takes a deep breath. "Would you like a scone before you finish that drink?"

So this is it, our hero realizes. This will be his last drink. This will be the last time he eats a scone and has to think: Boy, scones taste like dried cardboard.

In real life, our hero can't get food properly through his system. All he thinks about is getting his wife back. Some days, he's convinced he is too sensitive for the world. Even though his parents were loving to him, he still walks the Earth as if carrying a terrible burden and he doesn't know why this is true. He has kissed every single goddamn photograph of his wife in the house. He hasn't just kissed them, he has licked every one of them, front, back, sides, and corners. And for this, he has paper cuts all over his tongue. This man is nothing if not paralyzing melodrama. But in the science fiction story, when asked what should be done with the species, our hero says without a lick of melodrama, "Burn the whole lot of us to the ground."

As much as our science fiction hero hated his father for leaving, he still kept his collection of stamps. This is worth noting. He isn't melodramatic on the surface, but he has carried these fifteen VacuSealed books from apartment to apartment, city to city, country to country, as if the stamp collection were a burden important for him to carry. These stupid stamp books he's never even opened to look at. Maybe he carries these fifteen books to remember how he hates mankind, or maybe he carries them to remember that even with all our unforgivable flaws, there is still something that we can't help but carry with us.

Our hero finishes his coffee. He chews up his scone so that nothing is left but a pile of crumbs on the table.

"So what did you want from us?" our hero asks.

The JuLef picks at the crumbs on the table and eats them. "The formula to free will."

Damn it, our hero thinks. He doesn't want a goddamn philosophy speech as his last conversation. A stomachache and a discussion about free will were not on his wish list. What he wants is another drink.

"I've refilled your cup," the monkey says, and our hero looks down to see the cup is refilled. This pleases our hero so much that he is willing to listen to a little more philosophical manure.

"Your species," the monkey continues, "actually chooses at any given moment what they want to do. They improvise," the monkey says. "The sad thing is that 999 times out of 1,000, they do what we predict they will do and they do it because of fear." The monkey shakes his head as if this were a new disappointment. "Your species isn't as interesting as we had hoped, but we will still learn from what we have acquired."

Our hero is skeptical that anyone could learn from watching Brando pick up a glove, even though he'll admit it was a charming scene.

"So are y'all any better than us?" our hero says, a little less impressed with this brilliant monkey.

"No," the monkey says and he checks his watch. Our hero realizes that the JuLef story is long and complex, and there is no time to recount it today.

"I guess it's time," our hero says.

"Yes," the monkey says. "It's time."

Our hero laughs, thinking about how hopeful all those Earthlings were that our hero could save them. That silly scheme with the neutron bomb. In a way, our hero is disappointed—he had hoped this meeting would inspire something different in him. Inspire anything in him.

Just then a song starts playing. It isn't screeching like before. It's a regular song. In fact, it is a song that his mother used to sing to him when he was a child. "Raindrops Keep Falling on My Head." It was the song he was humming earlier. How much he misses his mother and her soothing raindrop voice.

"Ahh," the monkey says. "They fixed it. We wanted to play something that would make you feel sentimental during these last moments of life for your species. This song is playing all across Earth in your honor."

The song gives our hero a strange feeling inside of himself. It is a feeling he hasn't remembered feeling for a long time. He wants to cry. Not because he is sad. But because he just wants to cry.

"We have always liked you," the JuLef says, "and we wanted to make you more comfortable in these last few seconds than the stinky mess of your species." Although our hero isn't impressed with his own species, he doesn't often think of them as stinky. It is the JuLef species that stinks. In fact, they smell like the ass of a rat if you get in close enough. Which he tries not to do often. He considers telling his companion a few of the famous "Smelly JuLef" jokes that humans tell, but then thinks again.

The JuLef takes a moment to smell his own chest and shoulders and armpits and then looks at our hero again.

"We even thought," the JuLef continues, "to bring your father back to life, so that you could enjoy watching him suffer one last time. But we decided that that would be too ghoulish."

In real life, our hero doesn't get quite this much respect from his coffee shop companion. In real life, our hero's wife asks our hero to stop weeping. In real life, our hero is on his knees begging until his wife has to leave the café. The meeting is over within five minutes, and our hero is left alone again. He feels like a giant meteor has blown straight through his heart and lungs. Unfortunately, the real life solar system is not in the least bit of danger.

In the science fiction story, at the sound of his father's name alongside his mother's song, our hero is filled with a rage for this JuLef creature. He feels a lifetime of anger bubbling over. He hates this creature for trying to evoke a feeling inside of him. He is particularly offended that this creature would suggest it knows how our hero feels about his own father. That our hero would want his own father to suffer more, regardless of what he has done in the past.

Just then, the monkey sits more erect. He makes a gesture as if he smells something bad. He takes a few more sniffs. The air is still wrong. "This can't be," the monkey says with a surprise our hero has never seen in a JuLef before.

(To be continued…)

Chapter Sixteen
Life Without Her

This morning I've read three stories from the book my father got me back when he was diagnosed with cancer. One is about a man afraid that he'd be considered a pervert if he waved to the schoolgirls across the street. One is about a boy who can't stop himself from lying no matter how much his mother begs him to stop. And the other is about a man who isn't allowed to wear clothes or sit on any furniture while he's at his girlfriend's apartment. I wonder if my father read these stories before he gave them to me.

It'll get worse before it gets better. You hear that a lot, but sometimes it's still a good thing to remember. It took me a lot of days of weeping and pacing around in my underwear and staring at the phone and banging the phone against my head and cutting myself on my ass, until I finally decided, *mahspeek*. Enough. It took me eighty-six days if you want to know the number.

It's easy to realize this after the fact, but drinking bourbon and apple juice for breakfast every morning is sometimes a sign you're off track. The Cali King bed felt so big to me that I decided to pile a bunch of old pots and pans on one side of the bed to occupy some of the space. I even took to writing my own messages on napkins. And then throwing them away again.

- Spank me, Julia
- Yuvi's Bloody Underwear Sensation
- Yuvi and the Flaccid Penises

In other words, things have gotten adequately pathetic around here. And worst of all, I find myself missing BLTs far more than I ever despised them.

The news from the Middle East is as hopeless as ever. Just as peace talks were getting started, they fell apart again. Killing on both sides. Blame on every side. And it falls apart again.

It's amazing to me to imagine what it's like to live in the middle of all that. Once I asked my mother how her family can live there with all the craziness. "What you do," she said, "is just what you do with anything else: you pick your *tuches* up off the ground and you start doing whatever it is you've got to start doing."

And so, even though I live in the easy land of Portland, I pick my *tuches* up off the ground, and I start doing what I've got to start doing. I start writing articles for local magazines to pay the bills. I start writing stories again. I start working on my novel again.

I keep in touch with Shmen. He says Julia's still pretty shaken about the whole thing and I get silent while I enjoy thinking about her shaken. "Don't worry," he tells me. "I'll think of something to get you guys together."

I tell him there isn't anything different in me that would change her mind. I tell him to forget it. I tell him not to worry about me. I tell him that I'm fine.

I ask Shmen about his health. I ask him about his limp. I ask him if he's seen a specialist for the inflammations that are spreading across his body.

He says, "I'll think of something," still thinking about me and his gentile sister.

I make myself another glass of bourbon juice.

My editor said this situation might be good for the novel. And so I told her, "*Kush meer in tuches.*" When she asked what it meant, I told her it meant, "Thank you very much."

POTTY TALK

I was sitting on the toilet and pissing in the women's bathroom of the Righteous Room when she walked in. She was tall and she smiled like she already knew me. Her lips were full for such a skinny woman and I wanted that smile to last forever.

"Oh," she said. "I'm sorry." And left the bathroom so fast that as I washed my hands, I couldn't remember if the event had really taken place.

But when I saw her at the bar, I went right for her, as if I were a man with confidence. She was drinking bourbon on the rocks and so I ordered the same thing.

"I shouldn't have been in there," I told her. "I just had to pee so badly."

"Well," she said, "if you do it sitting down, maybe you're just right for the women's bathroom."

She was doing a crossword puzzle and so I sat there and told her about my urination urges. "I can't pee standing up," I said. "I get nervous. I try counting sheep while I'm standing there but it's not that easy in public. Sitting is easier."

She smiled and her teeth were bright in that dark bar. "Is this how you pick up all your women?"

As is typical with me, my confidence grows stronger the more I'm insulted and so I said, "I can tell that this is a clear example of anti-Semitism."

She drank up the last of her bourbon. "I wasn't in the bathroom long enough to tell one way or another."

"The Nazis started out the same way," I said. "First they criticized our bathroom habits. And then they nearly wiped us out."

She laughed. Which was a relief. You're not always guaranteed a laugh when you accuse someone of being a part of the Third Reich.

I asked her why she was doing a crossword puzzle in a bar full of neurotic Jews, and we both looked around, because it didn't look like there were any other neurotic Jews besides me. She explained that she was waiting for her brother, who was the real crossword puzzle expert. She tried to get as much of the crossword puzzle done as she could before her brother devoured it. I looked at the puzzle, dying to get something right, but they were all too difficult. Except one.

"Quinine," I said.

"What?"

"Used to treat malaria. 7 letters."

"You're good at this," she said.

"Not really," I said. "Just good with diseases. My people know disease." My insides clenched up like I was getting my own case of malaria. In fact, the excitement from meeting her would make it hard for me to keep food down for more than two weeks.

The bartender brought out a steak and mashed potatoes for her.

"So are you from Nebraska?" I asked.

"Now look at who's being the bigot here," she said. And I was sure it was over. That she'd walk out of the bar and I'd never see her again. But she didn't walk out.

"Iowa, actually," she said. Her hair was red and shined even redder in the dimness of the bar and I imagined the state of Iowa as red and beautiful and not nearly as scary a place as I had once imagined it. She had a shy smile and her look was no longer witty or sarcastic and I didn't feel witty or sarcastic either and I enjoyed all of the cute and the shy that she was at that moment.

"Please," I said, like some kind of idiot. "Do it again."

"You want to reenact our whole bathroom scene?"

"No," I said. "Just that smile. It makes me feel so tolerable."

She didn't smile. "You're cute for a paranoid, neurotic Jew."

And so I said, "You're lovely for a Protestant, Midwestern Jew hater."

And that's how I met Julia. And a few minutes later, Shmen.

Chapter Seventeen
Belly of the Horse

The barn smells like a wet horse. And it smells of horse shit. And wood. Rotting wood. But it also smells of tangerines, which, I learn, is one of Ally's obsessions. Eating tangerines every morning in the barn with her horses. I can smell it in the air.

If I have to remain a writer, then I wish I were one of those writers who has to go out into the world and do and see interesting things in order to write. I could meet a murderer or a preacher or a porn star. I could surf and travel and hike and, if I'm lucky, I could break my collar bone in a sports injury. But instead, I'm the kind of writer who is impotent, who pops Xanax pills, who hides underneath the bed looking at his wife's baby pictures while his wife is gone, out of the picture.

Today, Ally will show me her favorite horse. I called her about this in advance. I asked her if she was still interested in me dropping by. After all, she gave me the invitation back in Chapter 14.

"I didn't expect you to come by," she said when I arrived.

"Me neither," I said.

She sits on a small wooden stool in the corner of the barn. She's wearing solid boots and a thick, knitted orange hat, which I learn is another of her interests: knitting hats while in the barn. There are strips of various colors of yarn all around her chair. Looking at her hat makes my head feel cold.

I wonder why I came at all. I wonder why she invited me. And I wonder about the difference between these two whys. There must be a reason I'm standing inside my estranged wife's brother's girlfriend's barn. I sure hope it isn't that I want to get into her pants—though they are nice pants. Rugged gentile jeans. Perhaps I just want to get into her hats.

Somewhere, an old radio plays AM and the callers on the program are upset about social security and health care and immigration and welfare and of course, about war, about the trouble in the Middle East.

"Horses love politics," she tells me. Two horses stick their heads out of their stalls at the sound of Ally's voice. One horse is perfectly white and has cheeks so big that it seems like it's got four tennis balls in its mouth. The other horse is brown with a mane that is gray from age and it neighs before disappearing again.

Ally peels the tangerine carefully and the skin comes off in one piece. She lets the spiral fall to the ground. "You want one?"

She has made this place too cozy. It's too perfect. I look at my bare wrist as if I'm checking the time.

"You're not going anywhere," she says. She smiles. She hands me three slices of the tangerine, which I take. Her hand is warm and the tangerine is cold.

"There's a horse I want to show you," she says.

It's a fifteen-hundred-pound version of show and tell.

#

The horse is big and brown and chubby. Ally walks up to the horse and pats him hard on his big belly. I want to warn her that this chunky creature is much larger than her and that it could crush you before you could say the word *shmendrick*.

But, of course, we're on her turf, and a scrawny Jew has no business giving horse-related advice.

He is healing from a leg wound. The horse also has a brain tumor that will kill him in less than six months. She calls this fat horse Fatty Lumpkin even though that's not what the owners named him. "It sounds better than Howard, don't you think?"

I nod. I didn't expect to be so shy around Ally and the horse. *I'm* the one who's supposed to come up with names for things. She is the one that's supposed to be shy.

She scratches his neck with fast, hard strokes and the horse makes grunting sounds. I can feel a tingle in my own neck. "Come and touch him," she says to me.

I step backward until my back is up against the door of the stall. I try to convince myself that I'm not really in a barn with this big, old horse, that I'm just looking at a metaphor to be used for my novel. But this metaphor is too big and smelly for my taste.

Ally laughs, and waves me closer. She thinks this is funny. Bringing some suburban Jew into a horse stable.

I picture the way my mom teased me when I was scared of something. "*Oof!*" she'd say. "*Mah ha-ba-ah-ya?* What's the problem?" As if it were the simplest thing in the world, as if you shouldn't be afraid of your big tall Israeli uncle who had two heart attacks, a stroke, and speaks of the Six Day War as if it were six days of intercourse.

"Why do you do it?" I ask with my back against the wall.

"I love horses," Ally tells me, and she kisses Fatty against his neck. Her lips are warm, even though I don't really know this.

"I mean sick ones," I say. "Why don't you get a healthy one?"

"You're all screwed up." She says it in a friendly way, like she just complimented my eyebrows. And then she's quiet for a few moments.

I think about Ally's warm lips. And then I think about Shmen.

Ally takes a few deep breaths, as deep as the horse's. "Just because it's hopeless, it doesn't mean you give up. You'll end up like my ex-husband. Too self-absorbed to see anything around you."

I have no idea what she's talking about. So I nod in complete agreement.

"Come and touch him," she says. "You're not the coward you think you are." Her voice is throaty, and I wonder if she always sounds this way or if she just has a sore throat. "Come and touch him."

"What kind of coward am I?" I say.

#

His belly is warm. And his breathing is large. I keep my hand on him and relax just like that. His legs occasionally lift up, and then drop back down to the same place. It's either a sign of being relaxed or a sign of being uneasy. Each time he moves, I'm tempted to jump away. But Ally stands behind me. There's no way out.

"Let's take him for a ride," Ally eventually says. Even though I'm busy holding my hand against the horse's belly.

#

When we're outside, Ally tells me to hold Fatty by the reins, and Fatty looks at me, as if to say, *What the hell do you want?* But I obey, and I hold Fatty by the reins while Ally disappears back into the barn.

There's a breeze, It feels colder than autumn and my face itches as I hold this fat, dying horse, who looks at me out of the corner of his eye.

"What's it like to be dying?" I say to the horse.

Why should I tell you? the horse says.

#

Ally brings back her stool from the barn and places it on the ground beside the horse. But she doesn't say anything. I know what she is telling me. I've seen pictures of this kind of thing. But a man should be able to mount a horse without a stool. It is the child that needs a stool.

And so I stand on the stool. And from the stool, I feel tall. I can see how big this field is, and I wonder if Ally owns all this land. I think I can see a vineyard in the distance. I wonder if I can just stay on the stool forever.

But just then, she pushes me a little bit. Less playful and more like someone saying, *Get off my goddamn stool!* But she pushes me in the direction of the horse. This big, fat, dying thing with a saddle that would surely chafe me in places where I don't necessarily want to be chafed.

The horse looks over at me. He says to me, *Are you going to get on already?* He says, *Horses love politics.* He says, *You probably are even more of a coward than you think you are.*

I stick my foot in the stirrup closest to me and while closing my eyes, I push my other leg over the horse. My intention is to gracefully slide my other foot into the other stirrup, but I miss. And I brace myself for the fall.

But I don't hit the ground. Ally grabs onto my secured leg and she pulls me back on the horse. She manages to make this gesture look like a small thing. She also manages not to laugh at me. But Fatty snorts.

I eventually get my feet in both stirrups. I hear the horse say, *Hang on, you scrawny little Jew!* And then Ally pats Fatty's *tuches* and Fatty starts moving.

It's not a trot or a gallop or even a gait. It's more of a slow, tepid walk. But sitting on a big, fat horse feels like standing on the top of a thirteen-story building. I hang on tight to the horse's neck. I press my ear against his warm neck and squeeze him like a lover. I try to think about something calm. I think about Ally sitting in that barn knitting me a hat. I think about her tangerines. The air seems so clean out here. I take deep breaths and feel my lungs expand against the horse's body.

As I squeeze the horse, and as I breathe and bounce with this horse, and as I think about my new hat, there's something I notice: I'm getting hard.

In fact, it's the same way a seventeen-year-old might get a monstrous erection in class. And it hurts bouncing against the horse. And it feels good too. And as I begin to start the process of thinking unsexy thoughts, something awfully childish happens: I come in my pants.

And as I come, the horse starts walking faster. He even starts galloping. So I hang on tighter. And as I hang on tighter, he starts galloping faster. And so I hang on tighter. My pants are all wet and sticky and I'm still tingling. And then this dying horse raises his front legs off the ground, so I close my eyes tight. And that's when I fall off.

#

When I open my eyes, my head hurts and it's hard to breathe and Ally is on her knees right next to me. She grabs my cold hands with her warm hands and she looks so gorgeously sad. I can tell how wet my pants are and I wonder if Ally has noticed. I see Fatty Lumpkin in the background. He neighs. He says to me, *You'll need to do more than that to impress me.*

I try to take a couple of deep breaths, though it hurts. There is something remarkable about the air out here.

With her little frown, I can tell how much Ally regrets this whole situation. She will soon tell me she's sorry. She will soon tell me she's never seen Fatty do that. She will soon recommend I get my head checked out.

But I'm perfectly fine. I want to tell her it's okay. I want to tell her she was perfectly right to bring me out here. I feel better than I've felt in three months.

MEN ARE FROM MARS, JULEFS ARE FROM URANUS
(CONCLUSION)

Just then, the monkey sits more erect. He makes a gesture as if he smells something bad. He takes a few more sniffs. The air is still wrong. "This can't be," the monkey says with a surprise our hero has never seen in a JuLef before.

Even though the JuLefs can perform actions just by thought, even though the JuLefs can perform in a fraction of a second what would take us humans years to perform, even though this JuLef creature could simply destroy our hero the second he realizes our hero's change in heart, the JuLef leaps for our hero in the same clumsy way that an Earth mammal leaps for another Earth mammal when feeling threatened.

When the monkey clutches onto our hero, our hero still has the wherewithal to say, "Take your stinking paws off me, you damn dirty ape!" and he feels a childlike pleasure in getting to say such a line from such a film. And then, our hero lets out a stream of hot, caffeine-induced urine from his penis, setting off the explosive device which blows up our hero, the JuLef, and the entire planet of Uranus.

The plan, strangely enough, is executed exactly how the Earth leaders had planned it.

In real life, our hero doesn't get the opportunity to save the solar system. He walks home from the coffee shop with a horrible burning in his chest. But even though his wife is all but finished with him, he is somehow glad that he still loves his wife. He even considers writing a story about his wife and her beautiful giggle.

For a moment, he is glad to be able to have such emotions even though on some days it feels like he carries the burden of his whole species in his chest. The book isn't closed for our hero. And even though he doesn't know how to save his own marriage, he believes it is this tremendous emotion inside of him that allows our science fiction hero to save the solar system—other than poor Uranus.

Before our science fiction hero disintegrates at the center of a four-hundred-gigaton explosion, his last thought is this: I wish I had opened even one of those stamp books before it was too late.

Chapter Eighteen
Purple Monkey Dishwasher

When I get the call at four in the morning, I think: Dad. I think: Mom. But because they're dead, I think: Julia. But since I haven't seen or heard from her in three months, I pick up the phone and say, "Ally?"

"Shmuvi," Ally says in a voice that is too quiet and too awake.

There's a split second when I think about how she held my hand after I fell off the horse. I imagine her concern for me. I imagine how much she wanted me to touch her fat horse's belly. I think about that hat she might one day knit me.

And then I think about the actual reason she might be calling me at this hour. So I jump out of bed. "What's wrong?"

I'm holding my car keys before I even have my pants on. And when she tells me that Shmen is in the hospital, I don't ask what for.

#

4:22 AM

I get up to the fifth floor waiting room and Ally and Maddy are sleeping on one of the couches. They look so cute and comfortable. I want to squeeze in next to them. I want to cuddle. I don't want to think about all the things that I think about: the real worries and the fake worries and the worry that I don't even know the difference. But when I sit on the couch next to them, it is more complicated to get comfortable than I expected. Even so, I give myself thirty seconds before waking them up.

"How is he?" I ask. And I get two answers that make no sense:

Maddy says, "Purple monkey dishwasher."

Ally says, "Hemophagocytic syndrome."

I've always worried about Shmen, but it always felt like an unrealized weight, something that maybe could happen, but not something that I expected to really happen.

"It's bad?" I ask, guessing from the number of syllables in the syndrome.

"He's pretty sick. Do you want to see him?"

"No." And then I head toward Shmen's room.

#

5:22 AM

It turns out that Shmen isn't in good shape. He's running a fever. There are problems with his liver and his lymph nodes. His immune system isn't right. He has inexplicable inflammation in his knees, his neck. He can't see out of one eye, and his anus is nearly swollen shut. He's on some strong drugs and there are at least two things dripping into his veins. His lips look dry, and his eyes look wet, and I ask him what the hell is going on.

"I'm feeling kind of horny," he says to me.

"Shmen," I say. "It's Yuvi. How are you doing?"

"Shmuvi, it's you," he says. "I'm feeling kind of horny."

"That's good," I say. "What else is going on?"

"Well," he says. "It looks like my bike racing career is out the window."

He's mumbling the whole time and I don't have much hope of entering into his world at the moment. Even so, I can't help but try to fake some sanity.

"Your bike career was never in the window," I say. "I've never seen you on a bicycle in my life."

"You've always been such a pessimist, Yuvi. Have some hope." He takes a deep breath. "Now let me practice my moves."

And then he falls back asleep.

#

<u>6:33 AM</u>

The doctor says Shmen needs to stop drinking in order to survive this condition. He needs to get physical therapy. He needs to see a nutritionist. Before the doctor leaves, he tells us, "Joel is still young and strong but he needs to take care of himself better."

Ally's tears are quiet. Maddy's tears are not.

I stand there and try to memorize everything the doctor has said.

The last thing the doctor says is, "I'm dying for some Fritos before my next surgery."

#

<u>7:04 AM</u>

It's just me in the room when Shmen wakes up.

"Shmuvi," he says. "I feel like hell."

"You look pretty bad," I say. I can tell the world is blurry by the way he looks at things for too long.

"You don't look so good yourself," Shmen says. He reaches out his hand and I grab it. His hand is cold, too cold for

someone who is supposedly running a fever, and so I hold
it tight, trying to warm him up. It's sunny outside and the
hospital window is huge and I notice Shmen staring up at the
sky while his stomach grumbles. He stares in a blank kind of
way as if his dream is taking place up in the sky.

"Is it too bright?" I ask.

"Purple monkey dishwasher."

#

<u>7:14 AM</u>

There is a noise in the hallway. I hear someone calling out
Shmen's full name and this voice is awfully familiar but I'm
not thinking too clearly. Even so, I let go of Shmen's hand.

And then Julia is standing in the doorway and I suddenly
wonder why she hasn't gotten here earlier. She looks at us both
like we've been naughty. But the kind of naughty that can be
reconciled.

"My baby brother!" she says. She's been crying the whole
way to the hospital.

"Save me, Julia," Shmen says. "They've got me on three
kinds of steroids."

Julia hugs him for a good long time, her arms tight around
his body and her face smashed deep into his hospital pillow.

We are on the sixth floor of this hospital building, but
looking out the window, it feels like we're not high enough. I
can still hear the street noise, people yelling and laughing and
cars honking.

When the hug is over, Shmen looks my way and says, "I
told you I'd find a way to get you two together."

MY AH-VAH-TEE-ACH FEVER

It happened in my aunt and uncle's sixth-floor apartment in Beer-Sheva. My mom would take me to visit her three sisters in Israel during summer vacations, and this was my favorite of her sisters. This was the one who played with me on the floor like she wasn't an adult. The one who had a missing front tooth that made her smile so nice to be around. The one who always wanted a child but never got one.

Earlier that day, I was sticking my head out the window just like any boy would do with a sixth-floor window. There was a man on the street yelling "Ah-Vah-Tee-Ach!" over and over again. The echo of his yell made it feel like the whole Israeli sky was yelling this word. My mom wasn't around, so I asked my aunt what the word meant.

She said, "It is, how you say—" But she didn't know the word in English. And so she started using hand gestures, making a big round ball shape in front of her stomach.

A belly? A baby? A bomb?

"No," she said. "I don't know how you say it." And so she took me out of the apartment and down the street to see the man who was selling watermelons. The man's skin was the darkest dark brown I'd ever seen and the watermelon was the reddest dark red on the inside. We carried the biggest one back to the room and then dug in. She asked me not to eat so much, but she also enjoyed how excited I was. And, as if the watermelon was the cause of it all, I got a fever of a 102 when I finished with that thing. I got so dizzy she had to carry me to the guest bedroom, where I passed out for who knows how many hours.

The air was warm and dry in the Negev desert and it was common after a nap—even when you weren't sick—to wake up with a dry and dusty throat. But that wasn't what bothered me.

When I woke up, everything felt normal except there was a feeling worse than any feeling I'd ever felt. As an adult, I've tried to describe it to a million therapists in a million ways using a million desperate hand gestures. And I always get that same look when I'm done trying to talk about how it felt. So now I know: trying to talk about how it felt is nothing better than stupid. And here is how it felt:

It was like you had just peed in your bed. But I hadn't peed in the bed. It was like peeing but worse. That your pee had permanently stained the bed. And that it burned through the mattress and stained the floor. Permanently. And it made a smell that would never go away. Everyone in the building smelled that smell of rotten apple juice. And your parents hated you for destroying their furniture. And you would never be able to sleep again. And you would be followed by your parents everywhere you went. And they would be saying, "I hate you, I hate you, I hate you, I hate you." And it would never stop.

None of this happened. I don't think anyone I've loved has ever said the word "hate" to me in the real world. It was all inside of me. But I yelled louder than anyone in that apartment complex had ever yelled.

One way to determine the seriousness of your condition is by the number of neighbors that ask what the hell is going on in there. For me: six.

My mother and my aunt ran into the room when they heard me yelling. I was sitting up in the bed and squeezing the pillow. I yelled many things, but one thing I remember yelling without even really understanding what it meant was: "Ain lee tikvah."

"What is hopeless?" my mom said.

And my aunt said, "Mah karah? Mah karah?"

It was impossible for me to believe that they didn't understand the obvious tragedy here, so I ran out of the bedroom while squeezing that sweaty pillow. I ran into the room where they kept the piano and fell to the floor, smacking my hands on the floor while saying, "Never, never, never, never."

My aunt wouldn't enter the room. She was standing back in the hallway and I saw that look in her eyes even though I don't know how I could have seen her. One part of her was telling her to help this terrified boy, and another part was telling her to clear the blast zone. And my mother wasn't far behind either. She stayed at the corner, telling me it was okay from so far away. But my banging on the floor was all there was in my world, the chords reverberateing inside the piano.

I threw the pillow across the room and went over to grab it again. And then I threw it again. And grabbed it again. The pillow cover fell off the pillow but I kept throwing that dirty pillow back and forth. With my mother nearly stepping forward from the corner of the room, but not quite. And I don't think I wanted comfort at that point anyhow. It was the kind of feeling you feel when it's too late for comfort.

Slowly, during this ritual throwing and retrieving, I did calm. Without any explanation, the trauma downgraded to terror, then to fear, then to dread, and then it was just a headache and damp clothes against my clammy skin. All it took was time.

Within a few minutes, I had lost the feeling completely. And I only remembered bits and pieces of what had just happened. My mother was now hugging me tightly and calming me using all the Hebrew, English, Ladino, and Yiddish in her power.

I had no proof about what had happened, other than an overly dirty pillow. But I still have a touch of terror from that Negev afternoon twenty-whatever years ago.

#

Later that night, when my mother tucked me into bed, she said, "You had some kind of meshugas in you!" She smiled, but it was more of an exhausted smile than a good one.

"Mommy," I said. "You know that thing that happened to me today?"

She didn't nod yes, but she didn't need to.

"What if it comes back?" I asked.

"Chas vi-cha-leela," my mother said, which means something like God forbid.

After a few minutes more of sitting next to me on the bed, my mother kissed me goodnight and left me to sleep with a brand new pillow and a brand new pillow cover. And that night, I dreamed prettier dreams, with no urine stains in sight.

But before she left, I did say one last thing, which she pretended not to hear:

"I kind of miss that feeling."

Chapter Nineteen
Simple Swollen Anus

Shmen gives Julia an update about his situation. And Shmen has it pretty well together and speaks clearly and tells her everything. Except he doesn't tell her how he's horny. And Julia takes a deep breath and sits next to him and holds his hand just like I was holding his hand a moment before. She says "I'm with you" a couple times. And after a minute she looks at me as if she had forgotten I was in the room.

"You're looking well," I say to her in my best formal, detached, robotic, unsuggestive, strong, confident, *goyishe* voice.

"So are you," she says to me in a better detached voice.

"Thank you," I say, and I lift a pretend hat off my head.

Shmen seems like he is going to space out again, but he doesn't, he just waits and lets the awkwardness sit around for a while, and just before it kills all of us, he says in a violent whisper, "Jesus Christ! Would you guys shut the fuck up and get back together and start fucking each other and have a goddamn kid already!"

We're all silent for a while. I try to remember what it was that caused our marriage to get so mixed up and I can't exactly remember it or understand it. For a moment, I wonder if there is no problem at all. Maybe we got stuck worrying about a nonexistent problem. Maybe she could come home with me right now, after Shmen gets better. I wonder why it took Julia so long to get over here. The only explanation I can come up with is that Julia didn't get here earlier because she wasn't at her apartment all night.

"It's not that simple," I say to Shmen.

"It's not," she says.

It's a nice feeling to be on the same side as Julia, as we try to persuade Shmen that our relationship is a mess.

"Yes it is that goddamn simple," Shmen says. "At least your anus isn't swollen and you don't need steroids and you have a working digestive system."

He has a point. My intestines are a lot more capable than his. I have no answer for him. And Julia doesn't either. And Julia looks at me and I see that same sweetness inside of her like in the olden days, even if she keeps her protected expression on at the same time, and I hope she sees something decent inside of me too. But there's nothing to say. It's the wrong time to say anything. Right now, it's about Shmen, and we shouldn't let Shmen trick us into worrying about ourselves.

But I get stuck worrying about ourselves. And so I kiss Shmen on the forehead and tell him that I'm off to get a cup of coffee.

#

Shmen does start improving as the day progresses. The steroids bring down the swelling all over his body. And it's pretty thrilling to see him coming back from the dead. He complains as they take him off the painkillers, but you can tell that he's glad to have his normal sense of the world back, even if he does try once or twice to get a few prescriptions he doesn't really need. I take that as a sign that he's becoming himself again.

While the nurse checks Shmen's vitals, the rest of us sneak out of the room and plan how we're going to force Shmen to get back on track. Ally will make him go to his various doctors. Julia will force him to perform his physical therapy. And I will force him to eat better and drink less. We talk about Shmen as if he's a childish *shmendrik* and I want to protest. But I'm also scared about what will happen if we don't do it this way.

Julia and I are cordial to each other, though it's not easy. Every minute the feeling is different. I either want to hug her or give her a good kick in the face. Sometimes two kicks. And sometimes two hugs.

The doctor says he's lucky he didn't die this time and that his life expectancy can either be a little shorter than average or a lot shorter, depending on how he plays it. The doctor then takes off to get more Fritos.

Before they release him from the hospital, I go back into the room to say goodbye to Shmen. I tell him that I'll be visiting him at home soon. And that I'm going to force him to stay in better health once he gets out.

"Okay," he says with too much enthusiasm. "Sounds like a plan. I'm in full agreement. Totally on board. I'm with you. Yep. I smell what you're shitting."

THE POOP REPORT

My editor told me to send some of my stories out for publication in literary journals. She said that I needed a more impressive publication history during this long hiatus between books. She also suggested that if I worked really hard, we could get my novel published in next year's fall list. And so I sent out that story I wrote back in Chapter 4, the one about Shmen's pooping problems that I wrote from Ally's perspective. And I got it published at a website called www.poopreport.com—"All the poop that's fit to print."

"If you search the web for 'Yuvi poop report,'" I tell my editor, "it'll take you right to my story. Isn't that cool?"

Responses to my story accumulated on the website. The first response was: "This story blows." The next couple of people also felt that it blew. One person said that it lacked poo-etry. But a few people liked it. One person said that the writer had poo-tential. One person—bless her soul—said it was sweet. And then fifteen more people hated it. And even though I billed it as fiction, everyone treated the story as if it were true and as if I were the woman narrating the story. Loads of people said that I should dump my deadbeat boyfriend and find a better man.

I was tempted to tell them that this was a piece of fiction and that they should stop giving all this personal advice. And then I was tempted to explain that Shmen was worth all the effort. And then I worried that I must have portrayed him inaccurately. And I felt like a terrible writer. And then I regretted the arrogance in me that attempted to write this from Ally's perspective.

My editor told me that sending stories to the Poop Report was as helpful for my career as taking a shit. And when I disagreed, she said to me, "Kush meer in tuches," all proud of her Yiddish research.

I was impressed with her for that—she was a more capable editor than I had originally figured. So I said, "Here's a more advanced one: Aht noheged kmoh safta sheli dofeket."

"What's it mean?" she asked.

"You tell me," I said.

Chapter Twenty
Telephony

I thought I was dreaming about another one of those forever-ringing phones that I can never get to. In my dreams, I always have some kind of disability that prevents me from doing what I need to do. If I need to pick up the phone, then I have no hands. If I need to scream for help, then I have no voice. But this is a real phone that is really ringing and when I pick up the phone, there is a real person on the other line.

It's worse than a real person. Her voice is serious and impatient before we've even begun. It's like she's talking to a credit card company about canceling her card.

"So what is it?" I say. I take a deep breath and try to relax my chest.

"I need a favor," Julia says.

"From me?"

"For Shmen."

"Okay," I say. "What do you need?"

"Can you take him to the hospital for his colonoscopy?"

"Yes," I say. "I'd love to."

She gives me the details and I'm glad to do it. In fact, I was already wishing I could be there for him. And I'm even thrilled to hear her voice. Even her cold and serious voice. I want to crawl into the telephone line and hide under her vocal cords.

"Are you going to be busy fucking someone again while your brother is in the hospital?"

Click.

TENSE

"Please, Yuvi," my editor said on the phone. "This is getting a bit ridiculous. It's a mess. So his wife left him and may be cheating on him. So what? You promised me a death and I'm already twenty chapters into it. I don't see how you're going to pull it off. There is no movement."

My editor was breathing heavily. I imagined her falling from a skyscraper as she spoke to me. She wants a movement. She wants a death. She wants a lot of things. But she doesn't want what I give her.

"The italics are driving me crazy," she said. "What's the point? They're distracting. And how do you sustain a slow-moving front-story with all that italicky whining about your past? There is no way you could sustain this story for three hundred pages."

"I take it you don't like it so far."

"It's all falling apart," she said. "And how come you've suddenly started writing all the parts with the editor in italics?"

"What about eBooks?" I said. "What about iBooks? What about uBooks? What about the Kindle? You're stuck on page numbers. Three hundred pages doesn't even make sense, electronically speaking. Pages are ancient history."

I felt smart all of sudden. Like I was keeping up with the times. Not that I really was. I had gone out of my way to find a cell phone that couldn't do a single thing other than be used as a phone. I had gone out of my way to avoid any references to technology in this story. I still thought of my computer as a calculator and a word processor. But when you're avoiding bigger issues, talking about technology is a convenient distraction.

"Do you even understand why you've structured your novel this way? Do you know what you're doing here?"

"Of course I don't know what I'm doing."

"And why," she finally said, "have you put me in the past tense?"

Chapter Twenty-one
Fuck Me

"It's not often that you get the opportunity to walk to the hospital," Shmen said.

And so we walk to the hospital.

We even have extra time to make the walk more leisurely. He's not due at the gastroenterologist for another forty-five minutes. And so we walk and we talk.

"Are you serious?" I keep asking him.

"Yep," he says. "Not a drop."

This is the fourth time I've asked this question. I've been having trouble accepting the good news. When Shmen said he hadn't had a drop of alcohol, I expected him to say, "But I've picked up a cocaine habit instead."

The walk to the hospital is about twenty uphill blocks of residential streets. There are dueling trendy coffee shops at all major intersections. I decide that my next failed book should be written from a coffee shop. Maybe it'll come out different—the narrator might spend less of his time alone in his underwear.

As we walk, I'm happy in a way I don't deserve to be happy, and maybe I'm this kind of happy because Shmen isn't limping any longer. He walks like a regular person. He looks good even. He looks great. He tells me he's started coaching Maddy's soccer team. He tells me sex is so good with Ally these days that he doesn't even bother masturbating. He tells me he only has to shit twice during the night. He tells me that he loves eating oranges cut like a grapefruit and grapefruits peeled like oranges.

I say to Shmen, "You were supposed to die in my novel. That's how it was supposed to go down. I told my editor that you would die and she liked the idea of your death. It would force me to have a story arc, she figured, which is something that doesn't really exist in my book. But I couldn't kill you."

"I could die if you want me to," he says. "It does make sense."

"Don't," I beg him. "I wouldn't survive it."

"But I will die eventually," he says.

"I know," I say. "But don't do it right now."

Shmen nods, and I feel some kind of relief.

"So have you talked to my sister lately?" he asks. "Am I going to have to almost die again or are you two going to get back together?"

"We haven't spoken," I say. Julia and I have been apart long enough that on some days, or at least during some hours, or at least across some minutes, I don't even think about her. I'm dreadfully accustomed to waking up and not having someone criticize my pantslessness. But the problem is that when I do think about her, it burns just as bad as ever, even worse, because things get more clear as they get further away. "I think," I say to my estranged wife's brother, "there's a bigger problem."

And just as I say the word "problem," I feel the earth shaking. I look over to Shmen to see if he feels it too. I've never fabricated an earthquake, but it seems like something I would do.

Shmen has both arms away from his body as if he is also expecting to fall down at any moment.

And then a full-size upright piano rolls down the sidewalk, heading right for us. The thing is half a block away and is going faster than a slow car.

"Clear the way!" we hear someone yell. "Runaway piano!"

"Fuck me," Shmen says, and he stands right there, watching this thing coming at us.

"This can't be happening," I say. But it is. So I grab Shmen's hand and pull him toward an apartment building. We crouch there behind a row of bushes.

Shmen pulls me back up so that we can watch the sight of a runaway piano. The piano rolls down the street and then hits the curb on the other side of the street. It falls over into a front yard and breaks apart with a tremendous and melodious bang.

"Fuck me," Shmen says.

We stare in silence for a few seconds. And then we start walking across the street. Shmen is walking faster than I am and when he reaches the center of the road, we hear the rumbling sound all over again.

Three more pianos all shoot down the street, and I once again grab Shmen and pull him off the road. They all crash onto the same yard. With three more melodious bangs. It's a quartet of suicide pianos.

"Fuck me," Shmen says.

Chunks of piano wood and strings and brass all over the yard. Some pedals have made their way onto this person's welcome mat.

"It's beautiful," Shmen says. And we race across the street to see what a four-piano collision looks like.

RELATIONSHIP TROUBLE

"I tried to kill him with a piano," I told my editor. *There was silence on the line—as there should be upon saying something as ridiculous as what I'd just said.*

"You what?" she finally responded.

"Runaway pianos," I told her. "Four of them. But I couldn't do it."

"Are you joking? Somebody tell me this man is joking." Even though we were the only ones on the line, we both waited in the hopes of this someone stepping in.

"Will you fire me?" I said. "Please?"

"You're doing this to yourself."

I'd been lost for a long time and it was not her fault.

We waded through our third silence.

"Yuvi?" she said. But this time it was her friendly voice, like when we first met, and not her why-can't-you-write-a-normal-novel voice. "Am I still in the past tense?"

"I'm sorry," I said to her. "It's not you. It's me."

Chapter Twenty-two
Israelis Are from Atlanta,
Palestinians Are from Cleveland
Part 1

When your brother-in-law is getting a colonoscopy, it's not the kind of thing you can sit and watch with popcorn in your hand, cheering on as the fiber optic camera explores what is on the other side of your brother-in-law's anus. So you go to the waiting room and you wait. Alone.

Alone is fine. You should be familiar with alone. You are no stranger to alone. But the hospital waiting room makes you want to cut yourself all over your body. It's a kind of lonely far lonelier than alone. The couches are vomit green. And there is a round table in the middle of the room with no chairs in sight. And there are two TVs at opposite corners of the room, up at the ceiling, and they are both showing the same nightly news with the same upset grandmother in the same old terrycloth robe crying about the same busted-up piano that lies crushed all over the sidewalk.

Even though things feel better for you, the hospital is the kind of place where your world is supposed to go from bad to worse. It's the point in the movie where some force—whatever it is—presses down on you to test your strength. And you are not a man of strength. So you eat your Fritos in fear of the whatever.

And while you fear the whatever, a man comes into the waiting room and sits next to you. Of all the vomity couches in all the waiting rooms in the world, he chooses yours. Part of you wants to thank him for the company. And part of you wants to run for the hills.

His skin is dark. Middle Eastern dark. Just like your skin. And you see that his hair—though much fuller—is just as blacker-than-black as yours. He's got thick black stubble, the kind that could destroy an electric razor. And even though he doesn't look at you, even though he is watching the grandmother cry about the precious piano, you know that all he is doing is looking at you.

Maybe he is Israeli, you think. Maybe he has a mother from the land of Israel just like you.

"Damn," the man who is brown-like-you says. "This room is depressing. I hate hospitals." And he looks at you, for the first time, officially, and he smiles a little, and it's not symmetrical—the left side rises more than the right—and you enjoy that.

And then you two make hospital small talk. You talk about food and bad television and dirty clothes and upright pianos and grandmother robes, taking good care to talk around the reason each of you is in the hospital.

His accent is only just a hint. It's small, like he has lived in the States since he was five. But it's there. And you recognize it. Or to be more accurate, you recognize what it's not. It's not Israeli. And so when he asks, "Where are you from anyway?" you get scared.

The response doesn't come from your brain. It's a reflex that is sent straight from the nerve endings in your spine. "Spain," you say. In some situations, you emphasize your Jewish background to the point of absurdity. In other situations you hide it at all costs. One part Fear. Two heaping spoons of Shame. Stirred in a thick sauce of Terror.

It's a terror you've had since you were a child. Even though you never talk about it, even though you've lived an easy and simple life where you can afford to write about piano collisions fearlessly in your underwear, you've still got this terror deep in your bones. Since you were born. Since before you were born. Your father had it growing up in the only Jewish family in the small town of Division, North Carolina, and his father had it living in pre–World War II Poland, and his ancestors had it in the pogroms of Russia. Your mother had it living in Israel, and her mother had it living in Palestine, and her ancestors had it when they escaped the Spanish Inquisition. And you. Even though you have no experience to back it up, you have this terror too.

Your brown comrade says, "So you're a Spaniard," with a little disappointment. More than just a little.

"Yep," you say with a false sort of confidence even the vomity couch knows is a lie.

"I'm Palestinian," he says. He says it so enviously easily. Like we're living on a planet free of prejudice and stigma and terror. And you see his dark eyebrows go serious as he says it. Like he has recited a verse from a precious text. But underneath the seriousness, you see a hint of his smile. Like he is experimenting with his stance on the issue. And underneath the smile, you see a little twitch, a little shakiness. Like he went through quite a bit to get to this point of confidence and his demons are not as far away as they might initially seem. In any case, you admire his confidence and you wonder whether you might learn from this.

But when he says, "I thought maybe you were also," you interrupt him with an unwavering, "No."

"My mom's from Spain," you say. "Portugal, actually. Right on the border there," and you point to a fictitious map floating between you two.

Where did this come from? You're not a liar. You didn't think you were a liar.

"Well, I grew up in Cleveland," he says, "so I guess I'm not really Palestinian."

"I grew up in Atlanta," you say, "so I'm not really..." And you close your eyes. Which direction do you want to go? How thick is that Shame and Terror reduction? You take in a deep breath and blow it out. Let the whole shameful world in and out of your system as this man waits for you to finish your goddamn sentence. In a regular story, this moment should only take a moment. But for you, there is so much space in this moment that there is even room for one of those italicized back stories that your editor tells you to avoid like a gastrointestinal plague.

ITALICIZED BACK STORY

Your first girlfriend—the Southern Baptist, the one who damned you to hell before and after you both lost your virginity—she was a beauty. Adopted by a God-loving Southern family, she was of Chinese descent, but raised with an accent that more aligned with Roswell, Georgia, than Shanghai or Beijing. But she had cheekbones that were higher than her pastor's pulpit and lips that were hotter than the words of God.

She loved you. You loved her. There was a lot of love in the air. And when she told you her God was loving while your God was vengeful, you agreed with her. "I'm sorry," you said in apology of your avenging Lord. And when she read you Matthew 21:17, you said, "Wow," in appreciation of her sweet-hearted Lord. And as you watched those warm lips speak those warm words, you imagined that they weren't just the words of God, but the Lips of God that you were watching. And wanting.

You asked those precious Lips to repeat the words. You asked her to press those moist lips against your neck as she told you the words again and again.

When she said that you two were destined to have four children and that you two would teach these children to love Jesus, you said that was fine. And it did seem fine. She was lovely and sweet and you didn't exactly have any kind of belief system in place. She had apparently done her homework, so why not go with her plan?

It could have gone that way. It could have been just fine. Except for that one time, at that restaurant, when there was some disagreement about the bill, and you two were apparently overcharged by the waitress. Your beautiful Baptist whispered to you, "That woman nearly Jewed me out of fifteen bucks."

You always loved verbifying nouns, but you'd never heard this one before. And even though you were not sure if you were or you were not a Jew, it didn't really matter.

Your response was just as idiotic as her statement. "Jew this!" you said, and you walked right out on her. You walked right out on those cheekbones and those lips, as if they had never spoken the words of God.

Chapter Twenty-three
Israelis Are from Atlanta,
Palestinians Are from Cleveland
Part 2

"Israel!" you say. "I'm from Israel!" And it's such a relief to admit this to your Palestinian friend. You think to tell your damn editor that sometimes an italicized back story is just what you need to push you to the next level.

At first glance, it's an expressionless face that he's got. But you look through that expressionlessness to find the expression. You know there is something there. But you still turn up nothing. He knows how to guard his expression better than you know how to pry. So you tighten your abdominal muscles, just in case.

"I don't like what Israel is doing with the settlements," he says.

It is like he is complaining there are no more paper towels in the bathroom. You can tell that what he is not telling you is far bigger than the little he is.

"Yes," you say, "it's a mistake," as if to explain that you are not in charge of the paper towels in the bathroom.

You feel some relief in not taking responsibility for the policies of a whole country—you've got enough shame when dealing with the policies of just one short, balding, Jewish man. To be honest, you are too distant from the problems in the

Middle East to speak properly about them. But you were born there. Your mother was born there. And there's a monologue running in your head that won't shut up: *It's messy. There is survival. One little country. Two little countries. So much hate. There is terrorism. The real terror and the terror of terror. There are policies and there is posturing. There is propaganda. There is history. So much history. A history in which everyone has been unfairly wronged, depending on where you mark the starting point. My people have died, your people have died, there is blood and broken bones and prayers and whispers and cries and bombs and bibles and betrayals and blasphemy and the smell of a camel shitting in the desert. It's messy*, you want to tell this man who undoubtedly knows better than you. But it's too messy to even know how to open your mouth.

You start to feel dizzy.

You can feel your heartbeat at your temples.

And suddenly, through all this mess, you notice that your brown friend has a gorgeous brown nose. It's crooked, just barely, like maybe it was broken a long time ago. And you wonder who he is waiting for in this waiting room. You smile, relieved when you realize that you don't have to talk about the Middle East right now. You don't have to say everything all at once. And besides, this is the wrong novel for that kind of problem. It is too big for this novel.

As you get lost in all your thoughts, you see your Palestinian friend looking down at the hospital's dirty floor. He has perhaps been thinking the same things as you, has perhaps come to the same conclusion as you, will perhaps save this subject for later.

"Mine is dying," he eventually says to the floor. "How is yours?" His eyes are unwaveringly brown.

"What?" you ask.

"It's my father. Prostate cancer. What about you?"

"Oh," you say. "It's my brother-in-law. And he's just getting a tube with a camera up his asshole."

Your friend laughs. He laughs loudly in an octave too high for someone with such thick stubble. He laughs like it has been a long time since he has laughed. Then he wipes his mouth from all the laughter. And he doesn't know how to proceed.

You say, "My father had prostate cancer too."

"Did he die?"

"Yes," you say. And you watch his face turn into something that is far from controlled. The sadness in his eyes makes you realize that he is as close to his father as you were to yours. And so you explain a little more. "But he didn't die from the cancer. He did well without the prostate."

Your friend kicks his shoe into the floor a few times. "With my father," he says, "it is in the bones."

"I'm sorry," you say, knowing that when it is in the bones, the war has basically been lost.

There is a long silence. A piece on the danger of bedbugs plays on the television news and it makes you itch inside of yourself.

"Tell me about your father," you say to your friend, trying to ignore the picture on the television about how to inspect your mattress for bugs.

Your friend gladly tells you about his father. This is a man who has been a mercenary, a pawn shop owner, a poet, a clown, a lion tamer, a mystic, a journalist, a therapist, a peace activist, a comedian, and a cancer patient. Your friend is a wonderful storyteller and, after he finishes, you wish he could tell you more.

"In his day," your friend says, "my father was a real mensch," and you realize that that is exactly what you wanted to say, except you didn't because you were ashamed not to know the Arabic equivalent.

You exchange numbers. You find out that his name is Yousef. His business card says that he's a journalist, just like his father. You give him your business card, which says, "writer, neurotic jew." You tell him that you're not sure about the writer and the Jew part, but the rest is all true.

"No," he says. "You are a writer and you are a Jew," and you're not sure whether he means that in a good way or a bad way or some other kind of way.

"We should do coffee," he offers.

"I'd like that," you say. And whether or not you two will ever meet again, you are confident there is sincerity in this moment.

You hope the very best for his father's prostate, and he hopes the best for your brother-in-law's anus.

His hand is warm and big and strong and you shake it a little too long and with that warm feeling still inside of you, you go to find your dear brother-in-law, whose rectum should now be camera-free.

Chapter Twenty-four
Off the Tracks

"Your novel has gone off the tracks," Shmen says. He mumbles this to me.

It's been a half hour and he is just coming off the sedative. He has dropped his hospital robe on the floor and even though he hasn't put on his pants or his shirt, he is fixated on getting his socks on, and insisting on standing up without help while doing it.

"What do you mean?" I say. "Why don't your socks match?"

I catch him when he loses his balance and he just keeps at it like it's part of his putting-on-clothes plan.

"Dark blue is close enough to black," he says. "Be careful of saying too much in that book of yours."

"How is your anus?" I ask him.

"It aches," he says. He closes his eyes and takes a deep breath before opening them again. "Let's go."

I hate to be the one to spoil the pantsless party, but I say, "Don't you think you need pants first?"

Even though that first sock takes forever, things move pretty quickly after that. Pretty soon he has all his clothes on and his eyes actually seem to focus on real things around him.

"Should I call a cab?" I say.

He nudges me out of the room. "No, let's walk. I have some ideas about your book."

"What did the doc say?" I ask. "Are you getting better?"

"Yes," he says. "Better. But too much scar tissue. They want to perform surgery to cut some of it away."

As we make our way out of the hospital, Shmen explains to me what they want to do. The problem is that the scar tissue from his many surgeries can cause infection and even close off the anus. The shit needs a clear path. I think to say, "That's just like my novel," but I stop myself. And I state my real concern: "Doesn't another surgery just create more scar tissue?"

"Of course," he says to me.

#

It's awfully sunny and there is a breeze and we're both glad to be out of the hospital. I want to ask him more about what the doctor said. I want to know more about this surgery. I want to ask him about Ally. I wonder how many hats she can knit in a year. And I want to ask about Maddy. She had a piano recital Shmen missed because of this procedure, and Shmen nearly canceled the procedure because of it. I want to tell Shmen about the charming Palestinian man I just met in the waiting room. I want to suggest we could all meet for coffee. But instead, Shmen insists on talking about my broken novel.

"I don't understand," I say. "I haven't even shown you my novel. How do you know it is off the tracks?"

"It's in your eyes," he says. "You give away everything. Your novel needs something else. You need to take it further. Have some testicles for God's sake."

"Oh," I say. I have trouble knowing whether his insights are brilliant, or whether they are a side effect of the anesthesia.

"Another thing," he says. "You told me that you were writing about me getting a colonoscopy, but that's impossible without me even having a colon to oscopize!"

"Oh," I say. I had forgotten that I told him so much about

my novel. But he's right just the same.

"You can call it a scope of some kind, but without a colon, they aren't going to get much further than my J Pouch without some real damage to my small intestine."

"Oh," I say.

He looks at me for a little too long. It reminds me of how my first therapist looked at me on my first visit. As if she were digging deeper into my heart with each breath.

"You know," Shmen finally says. "You look different." He takes a deep breath. "What happened to you?"

"I'm going to need to think about all this," I say. "Maybe we can talk about something else."

I put my hand in my pocket and hold onto Yousef's business card. I wonder if we'll really catch up again someday. A Jew and a Palestinian walk into a bar...

"Okay," he says. "But remember that it can sometimes get worse before it gets better."

"What does that even mean?" I say.

"Nothing...yet."

We come around to the block where the pianos attacked us, but all the crushed pianos are suspiciously gone—not even one piano key on the ground. I look around, expecting to see a sad grandmother or a camera crew or a crime scene with piano-shaped chalk drawings on the ground, but there's nothing, no proof it ever happened.

After a long period of silence, Shmen says in a whisper, "Did you think about your father while you were in the hospital?"

I don't say a word.

He puts his arm around my shoulder. "It's okay," this man with no colon and a sore anus says to me, "you're just having a rough day."

SKETCH OF A PROSTATE

It was two in the morning and I was staying at my folks' place when my father called from his hospital room. My mother and I each picked up different telephones at the same time to hear my seventy-five-year-old father cry out, "I farted!"

Although my family is not shy when it comes to the various forms of potty talk, this announcement was more serious than usual. My father was in the hospital after his prostatectomy, in pain, waiting for his digestive tract to restart after the shock it had experienced from having a nearby organ removed. I empathized with his traumatized organs, but I couldn't bear to watch how my father squeezed his eyes shut and made fists while waiting for the pain to go away. The nurse finally convinced me at midnight that there was nothing to be done, that he would get through this period, that it wasn't so risky even if it looked bad, and that I should go home and get some sleep.

I was thirty years old and still living in Atlanta, my hometown—my parents were in the suburbs (near all the best hospitals) and I lived in town (near all the best bars), except around the time of my father's surgery, when I stayed in my childhood bedroom with the Jimi Hendrix and Pink Floyd posters still on the wall. But now they were next to piles of my father's surplus of chemistry books—after a fifty-year career as a chemistry professor. At night, I thumbed through his pile of books. The books were in order of when he used them, from what I could tell.

On the day he told me he had cancer, I was over at their place doing a load of laundry. I was walking through the living room when I saw him quietly sitting on the couch with a three-olive martini and a big smile. He spoke about the cancer as if he were talking about candy.

"You're fucking with me."

His smile was too large and too genuine for any kind of joke.

#

When my father had heart surgery, twenty years prior, I was at sleep-away camp. They didn't tell me about the event until after it had happened. I pretended to be upset they didn't tell me in advance, upset they didn't pull me out of camp, worried about my poor father. But I was secretly glad to have missed the show. After all, I got a chance to make out with a girl for the first time at that camp. It would have been somewhere between boring as hell and terrifying to be in that hospital eating stale tacos from the cafeteria while they cracked open my father's ribs and re-plumbed his heart with veins from his legs. But as it happened, with my parents not telling me about it in advance, they relieved me from having to confront this truth. And besides, I'd never again get a chance to kiss a girl with a glass eye and the most beautiful fake green iris.

#

My father sipped his martini nice and slow. Like he had all the time in the world, like he was proud of himself for getting cancer, like he had gotten the Nobel Prize in chemistry. I stepped over my dirty laundry and sat on the coffee table, facing my father.

"When did you find out? How big is it? What are they going to do?" I wanted to know numbers and stats.

"Today," he said slowly. "They told me in the morning."

"My God," I said. "How bad is it?"

"It's bad," he said. "It's the fastest kind."

So much pride about his precious uncontrollable cell growth.

"But," my father continued, "they've found it early. So they're going to rip out my prostate while they can." He made a clawing gesture.

What I did at that moment was get on the floor and begin folding my clothes. I folded my dirty underwear while my father spoke with fascination about the procedure.

"Aren't you scared?" I asked without looking at him, speaking more to my dirty underwear.

I could hear my father chewing an olive, as if my question were meant for another man, but he wasn't scared at all. In fact, he took it as great news. At least now he knew why he was pissing in his pants at night, why it hurt to piss during the day, why he ached so badly in his gut. He said that after the heart surgery he felt like he was living on borrowed time. He had recently been feeling like his time had come.

"Time has come?" I yelled at him. "What kind of attitude is that?"

"Yuvi," he said in the sweetest possible way, "calm yourself. This thing is inside of me. Not you."

#

The night before the surgery, he walked into my room while I was trying to write a story about him. I had gotten past the point of resenting my father for any mistakes he made as I was growing up. But I hadn't yet filled that resentment with something else. So I sat there alone with no idea what I wanted to say.

"What are you writing?" my father said.

"Oh," I said. "Nothing." I instinctively covered my page with my hand, as if there were something bad on the page. As if there were anything at all on the page.

"It gets easier," he said.

"The writing?" I said.

"No."

"Life?" I tried. I don't know if I was serious or joking.

"Not that either," he said. "Life just gets worse." My father stared at his fingers as he spoke to me. He looked at the front and *then the back of his fingers like he was unfamiliar with them. I pictured this as a habit of someone getting old, something that only a baby or an old man would take the time to pay attention to. "You'll learn to handle things better," my father said to me. "Even the messy stuff you'll appreciate."*

He laughed for a while, I don't know exactly why, and I think I even laughed too. "Well, I'm glad we had this awkward little talk," he said, and he patted me on the shoulder and walked out of the room.

I didn't sleep even a moment that night. I read sections from about twenty of his books—some of the books I recognized and some were completely unfamiliar. The newest books strayed pretty far from his area of expertise. They weren't your traditional textbooks on biochemistry and organic chemistry, they were more like a study of the world cultures—books about Native American medicinal compounds and Chinese healing techniques and diseases that Eastern European Jews were genetically predisposed to and a book about the mushrooms consumed by the Inuits.

As I drove my father to the surgery the next morning—my eyes burning from such a long night—he told me that he'd slept better than he had in years. I told him that I read some of his books during the night. I asked if he had lost interest in his chemistry studies.

"It's all chemistry," he said.

We were quiet for the rest of the drive, but just as I was pulling in to the parking lot, he said, "Oh!" I was afraid that we had forgotten something critical for the surgery, like his health insurance suddenly expired or he forgot his lucky fly fisherman pendant, but then he said, "I got something for you."

He opened the bag he was holding—the bag that I thought had a change of clothes in it—and he pulled out a book: Best

Short Stories of 1997. I looked at the book for so long I nearly rolled right into a parked car—not that my father was concerned.

"I hope," he said, "you don't mind that it's used."

#

The instant my father was wheeled off to surgery, I started getting stomach cramps and felt a bout of diarrhea coming on. The instant my father was wheeled off to surgery, my mother whipped out a deck of cards from her purse and started playing solitaire on the waiting room table. I always envied how my mother dealt with stress through games while I dealt with it through my gastrointestinal tract.

Fifteen minutes of silence went by, the two of us the only ones in the room. My mother played solitaire like that was her main reason for coming to the hospital—Kings in the Corner, Klondike, Freecell, Pyramid, Black Widow. I began reading the book my father had gotten me. My dad was into giant books, giant books with scientific formulas and well-researched studies and historical facts, so it was flattering to think he had gone out of his way to get me this collection of little stories. It was full of odd tales, mostly interesting, about drunk acupuncturists and talking buildings and edible mushrooms. And then I got to a cancer story, an old man that dies of prostate cancer, and I got stuck. I had read the same paragraph forty times without comprehending a word.

"Mom?" I said as I sat at the table next to her.

The sound of her cards slapping the table didn't stop. "Yes, mameleh?"

"What would you do if Dad died?"

"Chas vi-cha-lee-lah!" she said to me, and she put the cards down on the table. She closed her eyes. This phrase comes from the Bible. I looked it up after my mother admitted one time that she had no idea where it was from. Abraham used these words

when he was arguing with God. He told God that he shouldn't destroy the city of Sodom, that it would be unjust to kill the innocent.

My mother opened her eyes again and before she started playing with her cards again, she looked directly at me. I could see in her eyes the prayers that she had recited, the quiet bargains she was making with God to save her husband. There was a whole world my mother never spoke about.

"But what if it happened?" I said to my mom. "What then?"

"Mameleh," she said. "Let's talk about then then. Okay? It is bad luck to talk about then now."

I had one hand on the table and she put her hand on my hand like she was trying to pick up a card and put it in the right place.

My mother thought you could cause death by talking about it. I thought you could cause death by not talking about it.

#

After the surgery, they wheeled him into a recovery room. He was still under the influence of the anesthesia and his false teeth were not in his mouth and he barely had his eyes open. As two nurses wheeled him into place, he reached his hand out in my direction and with the driest kind of whisper he said, "Yuvi?" He said it like he wasn't even sure who I was.

My mother held his hand and I pressed ice cubes against his dry lips. My mother blessed God, and I blessed the doctor. My father looked so thirsty and it seemed the water evaporated the moment it touched his lips. So I kept applying the ice, and I got wrapped up in it, like this task was pivotal in saving my father. Whether or not my father was ready for his time to come, I wasn't. I didn't want to have to learn about my father through his piles of chemistry books. It took the nurse to finally come in and tell me to stop.

"Enough," she said. "You're only making things worse."

#

My mother and I took care of my father during the two weeks he was recovering from the surgery. Every minute, I had part of my attention on that tube coming out of him, terrified someone would step on it by mistake.

This was the last time I ever stayed with my parents for several weeks at a time. I moved to Portland shortly after the surgery, and my visits back home never felt long enough. When the doctor finally removed the catheter two weeks after the surgery, my father and I were both a little disappointed that our time together was over.

"You're lucky I got cancer," my father said to me. He was wearing a diaper at that point, because it takes time to regain bladder control after two weeks with a catheter. My incontinent father was right. And for years, he threatened to get another disease so that we could spend more time together. "I've already done cancer and heart disease," he said. "Maybe this time I'll do diabetes."

And he said it with such joy. He loved the big diseases.

#

Sometimes, when I don't know what to write, when I feel too naïve to come to any insight or conclusion, I write down the raw details I learn in a day or a week or a year. Here are some of the details I wrote down during the month of my father's surgery:

1. My father loves to watch and rewatch the first Godfather movie, and my mother is attracted to Al Pacino.

2. 240 milliliters of urine can fill a pretty large container.

3. My mother, when she was a child, slept in a small bed with her three sisters and she had nightmares about cats and rats.

4.   In 1936, when he was seven years old, my
     father tried to dig a hole to China.

5.   The human penis, when it has a catheter
     going through it, looks as helpless as a crushed
     mushroom.

#

The digestive system freezes up as a defense tactic. Once it decides
everything is safe, it will start up again. But this transition
period can be awfully painful. That's what they told us and
that's how it went for my father right after the surgery. And then
my father farted and that was that. He told me that when he
farted, it felt like the whole world opened up for him. It felt like
the pain in his gut had been with him forever. Even though he
never kept kosher (a bacon lover from the beginning), he said it
was like every un-kosher thing he had ever eaten in his life was
stuck inside of him, every resentment and nasty feeling. And
then he farted. And the fight was over. He told me he farted so
loud that the nurses on duty asked for his autograph afterward.

But before this fart, he was an unhappy man. He pressed
on his gut and his eyes were shut tight and he was groaning in
a way I couldn't stand to hear. He had a little button to release
morphine into his blood and even though the drug affected him,
his pain didn't go away, it just got more abstract.

Without any morphine, he said: "They should've killed me in
that operating room."

With one dose, it was: "I'm a slave to their science."

And with two doses, he said to us: "All these years and we're
still wandering in the desert."

Book 4

MARS

Chapter Twenty-five
Stalking

So here's what I do: I look up Yousef's address and I drive to his house and I sit in my car, waiting. It's like a stakeout, except I don't have any reason to be staking out.

His house isn't a house. It's an apartment. It's in an old apartment complex, which is a bright purple building. I park in the lot a few spots away from his front entrance and wait.

Here is why I'm doing this: I have no idea.

Here is a more honest reason: Because Shmen told me to take my novel further. For a month I've been going nowhere with this suggestion and so I thought Yousef could help. A man with such a different background. It's *got* to help. My editor will love it. Maybe I can even convince Yousef to help me write a whole storyline about a Muslim character who bumps up against the main Jew in the novel and teaches him some insightful *meshugas* about some insightful topic. It could give the book more depth, more foreskin.

Here is a more honest reason I'm here: I'm lost and desperate.

\#

After four hours of no activity, I realize that something has to give. Jews don't have the constitution for a stakeout. I haven't even brought Fritos or coffee. And so I go inside the apartment complex. I climb the stinky, stained, old-carpety stairs and knock on his door.

#

The door squeaks open all by itself, like a movie door, like it's playing a part, and I'm sure I'll see a dead body on the floor. Except there's no body at all.

"Hello?" I say.

The room is dark and all the furniture is brown or gray. It smells of lavender or maybe sandalwood. Whatever it is, it makes the air feel thick. He is using one of those big, old trunks as a coffee table. On this table, there's a bowl of dates. I think about that *Raiders of the Lost Ark* scene, that poisoned date flying up in the air in slow motion and how we're so worried for our hero. There's also a black photo album on the table. The kind my folks used to have. The kind they had before digital cameras made each individual photograph so much less precious.

Beside the photo album are three 4x6 photographs. I know immediately that the man in these pictures is Yousef's father. He's got Yousef's charming, crooked smile, but he also has gray hair and wrinkles. A sweet-looking man. The way the pictures are laid out on the table, I know that the man is dead.

I didn't expect it to happen so fast.

I walk toward the pictures and pick one up. His father is holding a half-eaten green apple in one hand and giving a thumbs-up with the other hand. He's smiling, a delicious bite of apple still in his mouth. I look on the back for a description or a date, but there's nothing.

A toilet flushes. The sink starts running.

And so I start running. And it's not until I'm in the car that I see I still have his photograph in my hand.

Chapter Twenty-six
Sleeper Cell

On the way home, I get a drink at the bar, a drink that I shouldn't get because I'm supposed to be getting off the wagon, or on the wagon, or whichever is the one that is less fun. I hide in the corner of the bar and drink. The first martini burns in the best possible way. And the second one doesn't burn at all.

Yousef must have known that there wouldn't be much time left for his father. But still there is no way to prepare for it. He'll need more time.

It was stupid to steal that photo. I'm not a thief normally. Usually my problem is that I leave too much of myself on the table. But I love the picture. I love that half-chewed apple and that smile. I don't want to give it back.

When I get home, my house is completely dark. But I rarely turn off all the lights. Even the light that has a broken switch—the one in the bathroom, the one you have to stand on the sink and unscrew to turn off—is off. The digital clocks are still running, so I know it's not a power outage.

My first thought is: thief, burglar, rapist, terrorist, maybe it's Yousef getting back at me for stealing the photo, or maybe there's a sleeper cell in my bathroom. Or all of the above.

My next thought is Julia.

Which is far scarier to consider.

A FACE LIKE THAT (PART 1)

You drew a picture of your father once. It was a penciled sketch of a father and daughter walking through an empty parking lot. You're no artist—and it was just one momentary impulse to sketch—but this picture is as clear to me as any photograph. You in pigtails with each tail sticking out in frizzy balls that were so thick in the penciled sketch that some of it rubbed off on my finger when I touched it. I should have been more careful.

I wouldn't have figured that stick in your mouth was a spoon except that you told me so. The cup of mint chocolate chip ice cream wasn't even in the sketch. But your father was there—a giant next to little you—with your hand reaching up to hold onto his. His eyebrows were down low and he was walking ahead of you so it looked like you were being pulled along. You were looking up at him, or maybe you were looking up at the sun or some planet that existed outside of that sketch.

I was lying next to you when I first saw the sketch. We were newlyweds, or at least recentlyweds. Remember how the two of us would lie underneath that heavy comforter, the one that made getting up so fabulously impossible? The sketch was on my side of the bed, underneath the Kleenex and the aspirin, like this new sketch was already trying to get buried.

You were deep into some glossy magazine. That was your favorite thing back then, before you became so driven by your work. If cigarettes were your thing, then you'd have been smoking one right there. If you were in a Fellini film, then you'd be reading a magazine while tapping your cigarette against an ashtray that would have been between us.

"You were such a cute girl," I said. "Even in a sketch."

In a typical situation, it would've been a reasonable thing to say. But I should have known better.

The magazine went down. Your face came up. The half-closed eyes, the half-tightened forehead. You squinted at that sketch in my hand because of the way you have trouble seeing things after reading.

"Oh," you said. "That." Your imaginary cigarette: it got crushed into that imaginary ashtray. You turned away, you slipped out of the bed without the comforter moving a bit, and there was the backside of your body—so bright from the morning sun—walking out of the room, leaving me alone with your sketch. It was like you had to go, like you had something to do, like your naked body was off to the bank.

And I was left with the pencil smudges on my fingers, left with that sketch in my hand. There wasn't much else in the drawing, just you two in the parking lot with those parking lines where the cars were supposed to be. Underneath the drawing you had written the words, "A Face Like That."

Chapter Twenty-seven
A Real Man

"Julia?" I call out. "You there?"

No answer.

"*Ani poh-ched*," I whisper, which is what I would say to my mom when I was scared in my crib. But my crib is now bigger and darker and potentially full of redheaded gentiles. Not the kind of thing a mom prepares you for.

It's dusk. The world outside is so full of shadows and my throat burns and I can't remember how many times I've called out for her. This is how it goes in my bad dreams—for years it's been the same way. The world is too dark, my voice doesn't work, the shadows cover up the things making the shadows. Sometimes the things themselves no longer exist: it's just shadows. And then sometimes I see someone dead in my dreams. Usually my father. The skin and body look alive, but all the important things are gone. And when I wake up from these dreams, my throat aches and I have to remember who and what I am.

In real life, in my dark house, I see that Julia is on my bed. She is curled up in the fetal position. This is in real life. My estranged wife is in a t-shirt and shorts and curled up in the bed that we used to share. Right next to all the pots and pans I put on the bed to replace her. And I can see Julia clearly, even in the dark, her beautiful, gentile skin. A bright spot in the room. She's breathing, she's alive. This isn't one of those dreams.

I sit next to her. She doesn't move. But when I touch her, real gently on the back, her body somehow shakes my hand off of her.

"Don't touch," she says through her clogged nose.

"What is it?"

"Fuck you," she says. "You probably hate me."

I think about this for a minute. I can think of a boatload of arguments; there were fights, annoyances, secrets. Deception. Frustration. Communication issues. Impotence. But no hate. Maybe it's the clarity of the darkness, but all I see is two crooked people who still care for each other.

"No hate," I say. I rub her back and she lets me this time. I want to say the word "love" out loud, but it still doesn't come, so I have to settle for the negation of hate.

"Julia," I say. "You left me, remember?" There is snot all over her face and when I reach to caress, to get my hand right in the snotty mess, she grabs my hand and pushes it away. She won't look at me, and I know she doesn't want me to look at her. Even so, I can't stop looking at her, the way it seems that her cheekbone is trembling underneath her skin.

"I have something to tell you," she says. "And you're not going to like it."

I already know what it is that she's going to tell me. The way she doesn't look at me. The way I can sense the burden in her bones. I know it before she needs to say anything. My staring at her only adds to the shame she feels. I saw it in the hospital and I see it here and even though I don't usually know the difference between my worries and reality, this time I know that they are the same thing.

So I look away. I look down on the floor. At that pile of scattered papers. It's my novel. Or my non-novel. Or whatever it is that you call all that stuff that I write every day. Last week my editor said it was "even worse than desperate." Some days, it's just me talking to the people who can't (or don't/won't) talk to me anymore.

I'm not surprised when my wife tells me that she's slept with another man. Not a fake napkin man. A real man this time. With two strong arms. A full head of hair. And—I assume—an enormous, uncircumcised cock.

A FACE LIKE THAT (PART 2)

It was a week later when I found the sketch in the trash can. I knew it would make it to the trash eventually, and so I waited, patiently, for it to arrive. I'm a man who looks in the garbage for insight.

I placed the sketch between two clean pieces of clear plastic and kept it under the bed so you wouldn't be able to throw it away again.

Your father had taken you to the mall for ice cream. I knew at least that. But there was more.

The ice cream was too cold and it hurt your teeth and you asked him why ice cream had to be so cold, and he said because it's ice and ice has to be cold. And you asked why does ice have to be cold and he said, "Just because," but he said it like he had coughed up something solid.

When you looked up at him, you expected to see his mean eyebrows, but he was smiling one of those gorgeous sneaky smiles that you loved to see. This was common: to find him beautiful and scary at the same time.

But it turns out he wasn't even looking at you, he was looking at a woman with high heels and a tight red skirt and a hoop in each ear as big as your head. She was smiling at him too. Neither of them said anything, but when she walked past, it smelled like your favorite kind of Hubba Bubba bubble gum, the one your dad said was so bad for you.

You asked him why he was smiling like that and why she was smiling like that and if he knew her from somewhere. Without answering your questions, he said that if you don't learn how to smile then nobody will want to be with you.

And you wondered what that had to do with him smiling at this woman and you wondered what he meant by "nobody will want to be with you." But you didn't look up at him because you knew you had done something that you weren't supposed to do and your face was hot from his staring at you.

And then he said in the cruel way he could say things, "Especially with a face like that."

Chapter Twenty-eight
Off with the Pots

Here's the deal. When Julia tells me that she's been sleeping with another man, I don't like it. But when I see how close she is to crying. When I see how ashamed she is. When I look at her beautiful face. There's no anger. For a goddamn instant, I'm not dwelling on myself. I hold onto her, and I tell her it's okay. I tell her I made plenty of mistakes that got us to this point just the same. I tell her I'm not offended that she went off with a beautiful gentile man.

"How did you know he was gentile?" she asks.

I smile at her and her look reminds me of the way she used to look at me when we first met. "You have that *goyishe* smell to you."

In fact, I feel more affection for Julia than I've ever felt. And I don't know what to do with the feeling because I'm scared it'll go away. It feels so clean. I'm almost tempted to ask her to do this to me again so that she can come back again and I can feel this clean feeling again.

"It's darker than you realize," she says.

"What?" I say. "What's darker?" And I look around the room so that I can ground myself on a particular object. I look down at the floor at the pages of my novel.

"Me," she says. She pauses for too long. "I'm so insecure."

I don't expect this. I picture her occasionally frustrated and never insecure. I want to ask her more. I wonder if I should look again at her sketch of her and her father. Perhaps there was anger on her face too.

Her breathing isn't right. Her hands are shaking. "I hated him for cheating on my mother," she says. "And now I'm no better."

I'm sitting up on the bed and Julia lies down on my lap and I put one arm around her and rub her shoulder. "Your father," I say, "deceived your mother for years and then left his family without an explanation. That's a lot different." I find a knot in her shoulder and press on it to get the muscle to relax. "We've got some cleaning up to do, but it's not such a long way for us to get back on the bus."

"What bus?" she says with a seriousness that has no room for my terrible metaphors.

"I just mean we can still fix things if you want to."

"Do you want to?" She's as small as the little girl in her sketch.

I rub my knuckles softly against her cheeks. And then she looks up at me so sweetly. She reaches a hand up to my face and gently rubs her fingers below my eyes.

I lean toward her. And we kiss.

And it's funny because we're suddenly affectionate in a way that we haven't been in a long time. We're like a normal couple.

But she pulls away. "I don't mind spanking you if that's the way it has to be. But I wish there were another way."

"I know," I tell her. "I'm totally attracted to you, even if my *schmeckel* doesn't always get the message."

Julia hops out of the bed right in the middle of my ridiculous explanation and grabs me by the hand and pulls me off the bed so fast I suspect she's saving us from a live grenade. She says, "I have an idea," and then she pushes all the pots and pans off the bed without asking why they were there in the first place. They crash onto the floor, on top of the scattered mess that is my novel.

"First of all," she says in a big rush, "take off your clothes." And then she has to clarify: "That includes your underwear."

CONFESSIONS

Ezra and I were biking through the woods to the creek behind my house when I was explaining to him about the porn film I had just seen—my first one. It was at Adam Silver's spend-the-night party, and Adam had just recently found his father's porn collection. We were eleven at the time and the porn was called Secretarial Duties.

One thing I possessed even at that age was an awe about the way people behaved. Even in situations that scared me, even when I didn't understand what was going on, even when I was being betrayed. While my friends were fixated on using however many weeks' allowance to buy Pac-Man or Combat or Jungle Hunt for their Atari 2600, I was more interested in the way the cashier was staring at my friend's mother.

The scene I was recounting to Ezra went like this: the boss walks up to his secretary and stands silently in front of her. With a look of annoyance, the secretary says, "Can I help you?" The boss barely makes a nod, but it's enough for her to know to pull up her skirt and show him her vagina. The man does not say anything. He doesn't even touch this woman. But he drops his pants and ejaculates right on her face. She still has an unmoved expression when she says, "Let me know if you need anything else," and she wipes her face with a tissue.

On top of the eeriness of this scene and the other scenes, my main confusion stemmed from the fact that I had no idea what semen looked like. My parents' technique for teaching me about

most any subject was by way of giving me a book about it, which
was fine by me and often did the trick, but even though I read
The Origin of Johnny through and through and I knew that
sperm fertilized the egg, I somehow missed the messiness of the
act, particularly when it came to sexual acts that had nothing
at all to do with the origin of Johnny.

"It kind of looked like he was peeing," I told Ezra, "but it was
just a few squirts. And it was white. And it stuck to her cheek."

Ezra and I made it to our usual spot against the bank of the
creek and dropped our bikes in the dirt. We started skipping
rocks on the water.

"Are you sure it wasn't cum?" he asked.

"I don't know," I said. "It seemed like it was pee."

"Do you know what cum is?" Ezra asked me, and he threw a
rock high up in the air so that it made a loud plop in the water
when it fell in. And then Ezra explained it to me in such great
detail I wanted to ask him how he learned it so completely.

"Oh," is all I said to Ezra. And we were silent for a few
minutes. Me, because I had just learned one of the most
fascinating things about the male body I had ever heard. And
Ezra, because he was deciding whether or not to tell me what
else was on his mind.

A few rocks later, I found out. At age eleven, Ezra Roth was
so obsessed with masturbating that he was doing it five or six
times a day minimum. At first, he just did it at night in his
bed. But then he started doing it in the shower every morning.
(And why not?) He started setting his alarm twenty minutes
early so he could do it once in his bed and then once again
in the shower. When his folks went out—for dinner or to the
grocery store or even just outside to do yard work—he'd do it
on their bed, though I didn't quite understand why. He loved
almost getting caught, though he was still careful enough not

to get caught. *Soon he noticed that his cum went from clear and watery to white and sticky, but it didn't bother him, it just required a little more cleanup work, a small price to pay, and so he began carrying a wad of paper towels in his pocket just in case. He did it in the school bathroom, in the woods during recess, once he did it in the back seat while his mother drove him home from a piano lesson. He named the socks and towels and pairs of underwear he enjoyed humping the most. It was sooooooo addictive, he told me, the best feeling in the world.*

By the time he spilled out this story to me, he was nearly hyperventilating, and he was squeezing a rock so hard his hand trembled.

The thing about Ezra is that he felt no shame at all in his obsession. It was a very un-Jewish trait—just like his love of fishing. He masturbated like it was allowed. As a Jewish boy, you should not only fear God, who is, of course, absolutely displeased with you, but you must also fear the far bigger dilemma of disappointing your parents. Ezra was concerned with neither.

As Ezra finished his confession, I could tell he was hard through his jeans. And he held that rock in his hand and he was trembling and I took a step back, not knowing what would happen next. I was scared of Ezra just like the man in the porn scared me. But I also was dying to find out what he would say or do next.

Ezra took a deep breath, handed me the rock, and then said, "Look away for a second."

I nodded at him and put the rock in my pocket and kept one hand on it like it was fifteen weeks' allowance, but I did not look away. And he didn't mind. I watched him take off his shirt, unbutton his pants, and in just his underwear he stepped into the creek. He swam to one of the deeper eddies and his head dropped under the surface as he masturbated in that creek, only needing to come up for air once.

When I think about Ezra telling me his confession and then watching him ejaculate in a creek (that is now plowed over by the Tamarisk Creek subdivision), I think that I've never heard anyone more excited to tell me any kind of story. His confession was even more amazing to me than the act itself. I didn't actually think about writing it down at the time, but I did think about what it would take to get to hear more stories like the one Ezra had just told me. How many times do you get to see a storyteller hyperventilate?

When Ezra came out of the creek, he howled up at the sky—something that seems silly when I put it on paper, but Ezra in the woods often involved some kind of howl or cry. His voice was just beginning to change, far earlier than any of the other boys. This wouldn't be the last time Ezra was scouting out the world years ahead of the rest of us.

Ezra shook off the creek water and put his clothes back on, and we biked home in silence. There wasn't anything more to say that afternoon. I kept that rock in my pocket like it was an essential part of the story. And unfortunately, it was also an essential part of why our dryer broke that afternoon while my mom was cleaning my dirty clothes.

Just before Ezra put on his clothes, while he was still wet from that creek water, I remember hearing him whisper (more to himself than to me), "Nothing in the world gets any better than this."

Chapter Twenty-nine
This Is Normal Sex

The missionary position is an awfully crazy position when you're completely naked and you're not tied up and you're not being spanked and you're actually touching another human being rather than jamming your face into a pillow while imagining yourself being ridiculed by a gorgeous woman who loves to see you suffer.

I'm in this position because Julia has told me to be in this position. I'm naked because she told me to be naked. She is naked too and I'm on top of her, because that was her request.

But I'm not inside her. I'm just lying on top of her. And I'm so flaccid it feels like six Grand Canyons' worth of Viagra couldn't save me.

I see she has a condom on the nightstand and it worries me. "I love you, Julia," I say to her, "but what now? Is this where the virile gentile man steps in?"

She puts her hands on both sides of my head. "It'll be okay," she says, except with her hands there I can't hear a thing. But I can read lips.

"Julia?" I say with my voice echoing inside my head. "Did your gentile use a condom?"

She lets go of my head and closes her eyes. I can see she is trying not to cry. "Yes," she says. "It happened one time. We used a condom. But…" A few tears drop down her face fast enough that I'm not sure if I'm seeing things.

"I know," I say, even though I don't quite know what I know. So I wipe the wetness off her cheek and I try not to think about her gentile man.

"Are you still willing to be with me?" she asks, in a way that sounds like she doesn't believe she deserves me. It takes me some time to imagine that this is possible: that she could feel not good enough for someone like me.

I'm not positive whether she's asking about being with her for the rest of our lives or about me being on top of her right this second. So I say, "Yes."

And she nods. She takes a deep breath. She asks me to take a deep breath. And I do. And then she begins moving her body a little bit—how those hips of hers can move—as if we were planning to have sex.

And so I start getting nervous. I want to make it all good for us but the more I want to make it all good the less possible it seems to make it all good. It's like I'm giving a presentation to ten thousand people about my failings. And my vicious impotence. Vimpotence is what I would call it in my presentation.

And then there are other thoughts: of my father, how he became impotent after the prostate surgery and how I cared for him during those weeks while he was healing, counting in milliliters all the urine that came through his catheter; and I think of Shmen, who I still worry so much about; and I think about Yousef and his dead father; and I think of Ally and her hats, and the horse that I came on; and I think of all those times I masturbated while thinking I would never in my life have (or be capable of having) a lover. With Shmen, Dad, Yousef, Ally, Fatty Lumpkin, and intimacy problems all in the same room, I just don't know how I'm going to make space for intercourse and Julia tonight.

Julia puts her arms around me and brings my head down so she can whisper in my ear. "Tell me," she whispers, "some of them." The heat of her voice goes through my ear and across my neck. "Your kinky fantasies."

I pull my head back, so I can see the look on her face. "Are you sure?" I'm starting to sweat in the wrong places: behind my ears, on the neck, at the crown of my head. "Kinky is a polite word for it," I say. "Some are just idiotic stories of you getting mad at me for being a pervert. They're anti-fantasies. They're shame stories. I basically have a million shame stories in my head."

"Tell them to me anyway," she says. "Give it all the kink and shame and idiotic you want. But stay there," and she adjusts me on top of her just right, like I might slip off otherwise, which I could easily do, without anything really fastening me to her.

"Well," I say. "I guess I could tell you a little bit." But they're not the kind of stories that would be fun to tell. If I tell them to her, they'll be all shamitude and no sexitude. She'll be horrified and I'll be even more horrified than her.

"Yuvi?" she says, and she says my name so patiently and so sweetly that I'm totally not expecting the impatience and frustration that comes next: "Tell me your fucking story already." She flexes her legs underneath me a little like she's going to push me off the bed if I don't hurry up.

But there's some play in there. It's a game, maybe. But it's also not a game, because I feel under pressure to tell her something. I don't want her to leave. Again. And so I start.

"Well," I say, "I like to imagine you catching me doing something embarrassing. I like it when you're angry at me. At least in my fantasies. Does this make any sense?"

"No," she says. "Of course it doesn't make sense." She blows into my face. I smell cigarette smoke coming from inside her.

I'm convinced that this is a bad idea. There is something so risky about right now. With her. Totally wrong time for this experiment. But she grabs my hips with some force. She centers me on top of her like I'm a piece of furniture. And I start to get hard.

"Are you going to tell me your pathetic story already? Because I have better things to do."

SHAME STORY #11 (TELL, DON'T SHOW)

There are two ways for your wife to find out the strange little details about who you are. There's "showing" and there's "telling." Telling is where you sit her down and say, "Honey, there's something I'd like to talk to you about."

This is the preferred way. For one, it lets her know that you're communicative. You are expressing yourself in a rational and thoughtful way and this can get you some sympathy—even if your little quirk is unusual.

But there's another way for your wife to find things out about you. It can happen when your wife unexpectedly comes home during lunch to find you naked on the floor, watching a porn, with your feet tied together using her best leather belt, your hand on your cock, Bengay burning all over your body. And with an empty bottle of root beer halfway up your asshole. That way is called showing.

#

When someone sees something that defies everything they thought they understood about the planet Earth, it's a pretty amazing thing to witness. The first expression on my wife's face was joy. It was short-lived, sure, but it was there. It was the "Oh, honey, what a nice surprise!" moment and it lasted about as long as it takes for the light to go on after you flick the switch.

After joy, we quickly moved on to shock. This is the sensation one feels when the world is turned upside down. It can happen when you come home to find your house has been crushed by

— 222 — YUVI ZALKOW

a flaming meteor, for example. The shock occurs before there is any kind of personal connection to the situation—it is just a confused feeling, as if your inner compass has malfunctioned. I had about two seconds to sit tight in this phase before things got worse.

Then we moved on to anger. This is the "Holy Christ! My husband is a sick, disgusting, despicable, shameless, shameful pervert and I wish his parents never had intercourse and never introduced something like him into our species" moment and it isn't a fun thing to witness. Particularly if you're the pervert in question.

My wife dropped her purse. Her hand went over her mouth, except it missed her mouth completely and smacked her nose.

Now you should know right away that I felt horrible about this whole situation. I was ashamed of my predicament. I felt terrible for the discomfort that I caused my wife. I had utter affection for my wife. I loved the way she squeezed me tight when she came home from work; I loved the way she could imitate my father's Southern accent and my mother's Israeli accent perfectly even though she was from Iowa; I loved the way she bought me popsicles from the ice cream man when he went down our street.

There are just certain things that can't be digested properly. Things a human body cannot take in. My wife's brother doesn't have a large intestine and he must watch what he eats. If he eats cabbage, for example, his body doesn't know what to do with it, and it'll come out of his system undigested.

So there was my wife, frozen in time, looking at me, and here is what I said to my beloved: "Honey, there's something I'd like to talk to you about."

And on that note, my dear and patient and peaceful wife kicked me in the face and left the room. She kicked me awfully hard. I was lying with my face on the floor, still tied up with her belt. It was the kind of feeling where it hurts so much you can't even tell what kind of damage has been done, but you know for sure it isn't the place that is bleeding you have to worry about.

Chapter Thirty
Not the Worst Kind of Nightmare

After we have sex for the first time in at least three years (it sounds crazy to say that phrase: after we have sex, after we have sex, after we have sex), I tell my wife, "Wow." And she says, "Wow."

The crazy thing about the missionary position is that it is so warm and comfortable and nice when you're pressed against another body that wants to be pressed against you. I tell her that her people have a brilliant way about pulling off this so-called sex thing.

"It wasn't me," my wife says.

It burns in all the places where our bodies are touching, her breasts against my bony chest, the heat of her thighs, and I can feel her kneecaps pressed against my legs. We kiss while we talk. It's some kind of horrible, sentimental nightmare we're living in. But as far as nightmares go, it's not the worst kind of nightmare.

I say, "If it wasn't you, then who was it?" And I know my breath must smell like the breath of a man who hasn't left his house in months.

She spends some time thinking about this. She looks out the window. She looks at the ceiling. She looks at me. She looks at that messy pile of papers on the floor which I try so fucking hard to call my novel.

And she says, "The gorilla did it."

Chapter Thirty-one
Home

It's quieter with Julia in the house than before. I tiptoe to the kitchen so I don't wake her up.

I put my manuscript on the kitchen counter and I sit on a stool and read the manuscript while eating a BLT. With the lights off. Just the moonlight. And the smell of Julia in the house. And a thumping ache in my temples. I also put that photograph of Yousef's father on the table. It's funny. The more I look at the photograph, the more it resembles my father. Put this guy in a river and replace the apple with a fishing rod and it's the same smile. It's the same thumbs-up.

I don't know how much time goes by, but I'm able to read over everything I've written in this novel.

It's funny, my novel. I see that. But there needs to be more. It's me on the page all the time. I leave no room for anything else. And Shmen was right: the novel does go off the tracks. But hopefully I've begun putting it back on track.

My editor may never like the novel, I may have to take out a loan to pay back the advance, I may have to take an actual day job to pay my debts, but all those things seem like simple problems once I realize I might soon like this crazy fucking novel of mine.

You really shouldn't stalk someone thinking he can save your novel. Even though I got terrified too soon for Yousef to see me, I still suspect that he knows that I was at his house. He smells the cowardly afterglow of my Jewy presence. He knows.

Yousef must still be fresh in the grief of his father. I wonder if he died on the operating table just like I told him he wouldn't. I wonder if Yousef has friends and family around him.

"Still with the no sleep?" she says. Julia sits on a stool next to me. She's got something between her fingers and it takes me a while to register that it is a cigarette. She lights the thing and then takes a long drag. Then she grabs my empty plate and lets the cigarette rest on it.

"You smoke?" I say.

"A new hobby," she says.

"It'll kill you," I tell her.

"Will you let me read it?" she says, looking at the manuscript.

This was a boundary we had not yet crossed. It was as if my writing was nothing more than secret diary entries. Unless something got published. But most of my stories never made it out of the "maybe_a_story" subdirectory on my computer. And so she knew very little of what I wrote.

"I'm serious," she says to me. "I'd like to read your novel."

I think about this for a moment. I'm not talking about just a literary moment, I mean some substantial time goes by. Long enough for my wife to fix herself a BLT. Long enough for me to wash our dishes. Long enough for her to light another cigarette.

And finally, I say, "Give me a few weeks to clean some things up."

"Why wait?" she says. I see her suspicious look. She expects one of my typical, idiotic ways of weaseling out of things. Once I refused to go out with her and her friends until she pulled down her pants and sang "Raindrops Keep Falling on my Head." Once I asked her to put her hands in my pants during dinner for some reason that I can no longer remember.

I tell my wife I'm honing in on the core problem with my novel. I tell her that I see its fundamental flaw.

She looks at me for a good while. "Homing," she says.

"What?"

"You hone your skills, and you home in on an issue. But there is no honing in."

"Home, hone, horn, porn. Just give me a few more weeks."

I grab her cigarette and take a long drag. It's such a clean feeling. To have her cigarette smoke in my lungs. And after I blow it all out, I kiss Julia like a man with a confident *schmeckel*.

Book 5

IN THE END

Chapter Thirty-two
Yummy

Julia and I have gotten accustomed to being together again. Three months ago, I thought I'd never see her again. And now I feel like she's mine again. I know this assumption is dangerous again.

She appreciates that I wasn't so hard on her for her little infidelity, the gentilfidelity, and we've found a way to have sex, but there's more to a relationship than just fucking and forgiveness. There are needs and wants. She wants a baby. She wants a family. She wants a stable companion. She wants both more space and more attention. She wants to read my novel. I need to give her answers. We're good to each other again, but I still need to connect with her better. I have to decide about family. I know that subject has to come back around. And I still want to look out for Shmen. I still need this novel to go further. I still haven't had the courage to visit Yousef. I want to talk to him. And I still want to be spanked.

I've given you one kinky erection, one impossible colonoscopy, one missing prostate, some leather restraints, a whole mess of pianos, one ridiculous story about Uranus, a deceptive napkin, no shortage of *kahkee* and *schmeckel* references, a Palestinian in mourning, and even sex with Julia.

But that's just a list of my dirty laundry. Something's got to give. I can hear the clock ticking. Julia won't wait forever for us to get back on track. Gentilfidelity guilt can only be carried so many miles. And then real change needs to take place. And this novel will fall apart if I'm not careful, or if I'm too careful. I'm missing some pieces to this Jewy puzzle. And Shmen, well, I don't know how many visits to the hospital he can stand. Or I can stand.

Who knows how many pages I have left to clean this all up, but it can't be many.

I still look at the razor blades and think, "Yummy." Just a couple more cuts wouldn't harm anyone. And on some mornings—like on this morning—as I wait for Julia to get out of the shower, I realize I miss her more now that she's with me. And I don't understand why that is. I still wake up some mornings and think, "Shit. I'm me again."

I've also begun thinking about that gentile of hers. At first, it was relieving for me—like a hypochondriac who is blessed with a fatal illness—to know she fucked someone else, but the blessing has begun to wear off. What will stop her from going back to him and his healthy foreskin?

I also didn't tell her about Yousef. Because then I'd need to explain to her that I have been stalking a Palestinian/Clevelandian man I barely know and that I'm doing it to save my book. I've hidden the photo of his father along with my hidden pictures of Julia.

You'd think there would be more growth at this point in the novel.

As I wait for Julia's shower to end, I do something knowingly crooked. I call the brother of the person I really ought to be talking to right now.

"Shmuvi," he says. "It's you. I need a drink."

What I want to say is, "You're on!" But what I do say is: "You can't drink. We quit. It's 9 AM. It'll kill you. Julia will kill both of us. No more drinking. It's bad. We'll never be able to stop. Take up smoking or snorting."

"I need a drink and a sitter," he says.

"What's wrong?"

I'm wanting to know why he needs a drink, but instead he says, "Next Saturday night. We need a babysitter."

"I'll do it," I say to him. This seems like the perfect thing for me. "You mean with Maddy, right? You mean for money, right?"

THROAT CLEARING

I need to finish off this novel. And I think I know one way to do it. It's going to be a little bumpy. It's a long shot. But I don't have much time. It involves a pee pee scene, a few palindromes, several overly symbolic anagrams, sixteen clotheslines, another visit to a purple apartment that may change the course of a book. It also involves a small, insignificant mountain with a giant horse on it.

How many of you have I lost already?

I hate to think of it.

Chapter Thirty-three
Bad Dates

When Yousef opens the door, he is surprised to see me. Surprised, as in, he doesn't recognize me. He looks too sleepy for noon. He is red in the eyes. He has lost weight. His beard is too thick.

"Yes," he says. "Hello," he says, but he still doesn't open the door all the way to let me in.

"We spoke at the hospital waiting room many months ago." I take off my backpack and reach into a pouch and pull out his business card, which is all bent-up by now, and I pass it to him, as if that is some kind of proof. I imagine my mom saying, "Oof! Yuvi! Why are you so awkward when you introduce yourself?"

"Oh," Yousef says, looking at his own bent up card and back to my face. I see his mind go back to that moment. Back to when his father was alive.

"I'm sorry about your father," I say to him.

He is too dazed to know exactly how I know this information, but he appreciates that I've acknowledged it. I know this because he opens the door all the way and points me to the couch. I've officially been invited into his house, which is one notch better than last time. I sit down and he sits down next to me and lets out a big sigh. I put my backpack against my legs. I've got my mess of a novel inside that bag.

There is still a photo album and those poisoned dates on his coffee table though the photos of his dad are gone. I almost tell him that I was in his apartment three months ago but I can't imagine that going well: *Hello, grieving stranger. I broke into your apartment three months ago while you were shitting and stole a picture of your dead dad. Can I come in again?*

"Yeah," Yousef says as if we were in the middle of a conversation, "it's still hard without him."

I want to put my hand on his shoulder or pat him on the back or just express some form of guyish intimacy. I put my hand gently on the table.

"I know this doesn't help," I say, "but it took me some time to stop feeling like my life was over when my father died. It's nice to imagine that you can read some holy book or whack off or punch someone and have the feeling go away, but it doesn't work that way."

He scratches his beard and smiles, though I know he's not finding anything too funny. "When do you get over it?" he says. It's a question everyone asks—or wants to ask—when someone close to them dies.

"You don't."

He makes a grunting sound, which I think is good. I had the same fear when my parents died: thinking that I was supposed to completely get over that ache. But it gets easier when you finally just let it stay there.

"You want a date?" he says.

I grab a date and toss it in my mouth. I try to do it in slow motion like Indiana Jones, but it just goes up in the air and drops on the couch. And so I grab the date off the couch and stick it in my mouth the regular way. They are sweet and soft and totally not poisonous-tasting.

He puts his hand on the photo album. He begins to open it. But then he closes it and looks back at me. I wonder for a second if he is on medication. He's got Xanax eyelids.

"Is this a bad time to visit?" I say.

He ignores my question and keeps staring at me. "You do not seem much like an Israeli."

"How do you figure?"

"Well," he says, "you're too fragile and sensitive."

I don't know whether to be flattered or offended. Or both. Or neither.

"I'm sorry," he says. "I shouldn't stereotype."

"It's okay," I say. "When I saw those dates, my first thought was that they were poisoned."

Yousef smiles. "*Raiders of the Lost Ark*?"

"Yes," I admit, with my head down.

"Have you ever been to Egypt?" he asks.

"No," I admit, with my head down. I know the "Let my people go" Egypt. I know a little about the 2011 protest against Mubarak. But I don't honestly know what life is like in Egypt. I remember as a kid my dad telling me about Sadat and Begin and the Camp David Peace Treaty. I also know that Sadat was assassinated. But I don't know much else.

I can see he almost says something to me. Maybe he almost tells me about pollution in Cairo. He almost tells me about the beauty of the Red Sea. He almost tells me about the Nile. And about the camels that are sold at a Bedouin market.

"Never been there either," Yousef says. "But a great movie." I feel like this is good enough to know that he still accepts me, with all my ignorance.

We are silent for too long.

Just as I consider whipping out my novel, he reaches for the photo album again, as if that were his manuscript. He flips through the pages until he comes to one of a girl, maybe sixteen. It's an old picture, at least fifty years old, a faded black and white, only about two inches by two inches, with jagged edges. The girl has long hair, longer than the picture can show, and she is smiling and looking below the camera and there is a tree she is leaning against. A tree that is too tall to see.

"This is my grandmother," he says.

"She's beautiful," I say. And I don't just say that because it's polite to say that. I say it because his grandmother is smiling like the photographer just told her a fabulous joke. An inside joke that no one is still alive to tell.

"Yes," he says. "She was special."

He shows me another picture. This time it's his grandmother with her four sisters. And two brothers. And her mother. They are all lined up against a stone wall that is cracked behind them. In one of the cracks, a shrub growing out of the wall.

Here's the thing: her brothers are wearing yarmulkes.

"Your grandmother was a Jew?" I say.

WHAT TO DO WITH SHOSHANA?

Every day, she went with her father to buy fruit from the Arab man. She wasn't supposed to go. She was a young girl of fifteen. A girl who was almost ready to be married. She had no business leaving the Jewish part of Jerusalem. She had no business going to the Arab market. "A woman's place is in the home," her father had said. "A woman prepares for Shabbat. It is the man who brings home the food." But she pushed and she begged and she cried.

"What are we to do with our Shoshana?" her parents asked. Their two sons were strong, devout men, capable of becoming great rabbis and even more capable to work with their hands in the earth. And their three other daughters were sweet and quiet and lovely. They loved to read stories and were great help in the kitchen. But Shoshana. She was the daydreamer. Reading a story wasn't good enough. Baking the challah wasn't good enough. The Tanach wasn't even good enough. She wanted to see the world for herself.

They were poor people and they were tired people. All of them living in a one-room house and sharing an outhouse with four other houses. But an unhappy Shoshana was far worse a thing than poor and tired and cramped. And the Arab man selling fruit at his fruit stand was a nice man. A fair man. And not so far from their home. And so Shoshana's father took Shoshana. If it would make her happy, then it was worth it, even if he did it grudgingly. "When I was a child," he said, "we did not disobey our parents."

#

"Shoshi!" her father cried. "We need to get home! What are you staring at? It's almost Shabbat." Each time, he swore that this would be the last time he took her to see the Arab man. What a daydreamer she was! But she loved it so much. How could a father deprive a daughter of such joy?

For one year, they went almost every day to the Arab man to buy fruits and vegetables. This man had the best figs and tomatoes and olives and cantaloupes in the city. Even though this man's wife had recently died of cancer, he was still full of kindness to his customers. Every time they went to him, the Arab man smiled at them. They had a rapport with him. The Arab man told them proverbs from his world: the eye cannot rise above the eyebrow; your close neighbor is better than your faraway brother. And Shoshana's father told him proverbs from his world: don't approach a goat from the front, a horse from the back, or a fool from any side; may your enemies get cramps when they dance on your grave.

Although the Arab man was smart and he was charming and he was wise, these were not the qualities Shoshana paid the most attention to. What she paid the most attention to was the way he licked his lips between sentences. And the muscles on his forearm. And how charmingly he was losing his hair, a widow's peak, even though he was still under thirty. And she especially loved the way his face wrinkled beside his eyes when he smiled at her.

And then her father got sick. Too sick to leave the bed. And so he requested for Shoshana to come to his bedside. "Shoshi," he said. "Your mother needs dates for the charoset."

Of course, it took him a long time to arrive at this request. With his two sons away, he decided that he had very little choice other than to ask his tomboy of a daughter to help in this way. And perhaps the fever was affecting his thinking. "Go quickly," he said. "Hurry the way you would hurry if you were running home from the bayt knesset after prayer."

Shoshi jumped at the chance. She jumped in the air beside the bed of her sick father.

"Bevadai," she said.

#

When she arrived at the fruit stand, it was as if the Arab man had been expecting her to be alone. He wasted no time in saying what was on his mind. He handed her the dates, and he held onto her hand as she reached for them. "Shoshi," he said, "I want to marry you." His hand was warm and sweet and sincere.

Shoshi pulled her hand out from his grip, for fear that someone would see. And then she put her hand to her heart, the way anyone would upon feeling this way. With this beautiful Arab man looking at her. She could tell that he was stretching his knowledge of the Hebrew language to say this. She could also tell he had practiced this line a hundred times.

She smiled at this man and she said, "Eem loh achshav, ei matai?" which is what Hillel said almost two thousand years prior. If not now, when?

This fruit seller made a fist and banged his fist on his fruit stand with joy.

"But," Shoshi said, "I will marry you only if my father recovers from his fever."

The Arab man nodded. It seemed a fair negotiation.

"You must pray for him," Shoshi said. "I want you to pray for him."

"My prayers," he said, "are different than your prayers."

"It does not matter," she said. "A prayer is a prayer."

"Okay," he said. "I will pray."

They smiled. It was a quiet moment in this land, as this Jew and this Muslim stood next to each other, with only some fresh fruit between them.

"I must tell you," the Arab man said. "I plan to move away from this city. I will move back to Ramallah. And then to America one day."

Shoshana wasn't surprised by this statement. Even though she had no idea where this America landed on a map. Even though she knew she would probably never speak to her family again. She felt this was her destiny.

"What is your name?" this beautiful girl asked of this beautiful man.

"Yousef," he said to her.

Chapter Thirty-four
Ethnic Plot Device

We sit for a while, savoring the story. The story itself is great. But I also realize that Yousef is a great storyteller.

I sit up to stretch my jeans and say, "I've got something odd to ask you." I grab the manuscript from my backpack and drop the pages on the table. I let it hit with a hard bang. "Would you be willing to help me with my novel?"

I flip around through the manuscript. I'm feeling confident and proud of this manuscript in a new way. The words on these pages suddenly seem like they don't suck. And I'm thinking that with Yousef's help, there's a chance they could not suck even more.

"I need to take this thing to the next level," I tell him, "and I thought maybe it would be a good distraction for you as well." It seems like the perfect collaboration. Especially now that I see how this connection to multiple worlds is in his blood. This goddamn guy could save my novel for sure.

He picks it up. He lifts it up and down as if weighing it against all the objects in the world. His face gives away nothing. He could just as easily be investigating a cantaloupe at the market.

And then he says, "No."

I begin to thank him for helping me out. "This will be great," I say.

"I said no. I won't help you."

"Oh." All of a sudden, the cantaloupe turns out to be too soft. Or too hard. Or whatever the hell cantaloupes feel like when they're not worthy. What I've got on my hands is an unworthy cantaloupe without a plot.

"Look," he says. He opens the book right to the scene of Yuvi and Yousef in the hospital waiting room. I have no idea how he suddenly knows about this novel. Maybe when I was rummaging around his apartment, he was rummaging around my novel. "I don't mean to be disrespectful," he says, "but you're trying to use me as some kind of outsider who comes in to teach the main character a lesson. It's a bit contrived. It's like a high school creative writing story." He closes my failed cantaloupe and pushes it back toward me. "I don't think you want that. You'll have to find another way to save your book." He stands up. He walks toward the door and opens it. It's even worse than a NO. It's a NO AND GET OUT. "Anyhow," he says. "I've got enough going on in my life without being used as some kind of ethnic plot device."

I don't look up at him. I take my novel and quietly put it in my backpack. I quietly zip up my backpack. And I start to walk out of his apartment. Before he closes the door on me, I turn around and throw out another cantaloupe for his consideration: "Can we be friends?"

"No," he says, and then my ethnic plot device closes the door on me.

As I start walking down the stairway to leave the apartment complex, the door opens again. It's too dark to see him but I still look back up. He says, "Well, maybe friends. But first, figure out how to save the novel on your own."

Chapter Thirty-five
Palookaville Pee Pee Party

So it's not like I'm saving the world, but my first endeavor in doing something productive after too many months spent lost in my novel is to babysit Maddy while Shmen and Ally go to a big-screen showing of *On the Waterfront*.

"You're a lifesaver, Shmuvi." He grabs me when I enter the apartment and he hugs me so hard that my face is pressed into his shoulder and I'm worried my glasses are going to be crushed from his appreciation. I can smell a hint of alcohol coming off his skin. Or maybe it's my imagination.

After this display of affection, Ally's normal hug seems unfairly simple. "Thank you," she says. There is something sweet and something sad about her. In her hug, I can sense the woman who had me touch her favorite horse's belly.

"I'm sorry about Fatty," I say to her.

"I know," she says. She looks down at her toes as she speaks to me. "At least you got to meet him before it was too late."

"And touch him," I say. "And ride him. And fall off of him." I smile even though I am not sure if it is legal to smile when talking about a dead, loved horse.

Ally looks at me again, like she's about to say something sad, but then she says, "And wet yourself on him."

Maddy giggles. She says, "Shmuvi peed on Fatty!"

"True," I say. And it's a relief for me, because I don't need to wonder anymore if Ally noticed. It's better to know that you have every right to be ashamed about something. It's better than not knowing.

Shmen puts his arm around Ally's shoulders as they walk out the apartment. He says to her, "Now there's a juicy story for the road," and they walk away. His limp is more pronounced—it almost looks like Ally is helping him stand up.

After I close the door, we can still hear Shmen quoting Brando's "I coulda been a contender" speech. I watch Maddy listen to it closely. She studies his words more seriously lately, like she is trying to understand what's ridiculous and what's important and what's a little bit of both. When Shmen's voice fades away, she says to me, "Where is Palookaville?"

#

I make macaroni and cheese for Maddy and I have her sit next to me and tell me how school is going. But she doesn't want to talk about school.

"It's Saturday, Shmuvi! Why do you care about school?"

"Okay," I say. "How about you just tell me about your favorite subject."

"Recess," she says, "and then lunch. Now let's talk about dolls."

This is an area that I'm not so experienced in. But once she explains to me that her doll Dorothy Mae eats little orange pellets and that you can dye Jenny's hair any color you like and that Baby Betty really pisses and shits herself, I feel more knowledgeable.

Part of me is thinking about Shmen, worrying that things are getting worse and I haven't done enough to help. And part of me is thinking about that visit with Yousef, ashamed about the stolen photo and for trying to use a Clevelandian man that way. And part of me just wants to see this doll take a shit without worrying that we're watching her every move.

As I sit with Maddy on the floor trying to get her doll to piss herself, she says, "Why didn't they get a babysitter?"

"I am the babysitter," I say, proud of my promotion from novelist to babysitter.

"No," she says. "I mean like an adult."

"Well, I am an adult," I say, a little less proud.

"No, you're not," she says. "You're just Joelly's brother."

"That's it," I say, and I wiggle my fingers in an I'm-going-to-get-you! motion. "I know a girl who is in big trouble."

And then I chase Maddy around the apartment while she giggles and when I catch her I tickle her until she is on the floor laughing. Babysitting isn't so bad.

#

One strange thing about hanging out with Maddy is that she says the word "shit" just like it's a regular word. And I guess with such an advanced shitter and shit-talker like Shmen, it's inevitable. But it's still strange to hear it said that way by an eight-year-old.

So I tell her that she can say Shit all she wants, but she better not say Pillow Cushion. I saw this suggestion in a magazine while waiting for the dentist. Using a meaningless phrase is supposed to distract the child from saying the bad thing they won't stop saying. I even started using this technique on myself.

But after my Pillow Cushion brilliance, Maddy says Shit more than thirty times in the next three sentences.

So to hell with it, I figure, and I start saying Shit myself. And when she says, "Will you carry me? I want to be tall." I say, "Sure as shit I'll carry you!" And I carry her. Shit! I even run around the apartment. Shit! And she loves it. Shit! She pretends I'm her very own horse. And why not? I can be a horse for a little while.

I keep carrying her and she keeps giggling and there is this tremendous warmth inside of me. And it's not just inside me. It's outside me too. I look at Maddy and I smile. And it's not just warmth. It also feels wet. Warm and wet. And then Maddy says, "Uh oh." And when I put her down, I see that she has pissed all over my shirt.

Maddy goes into the bathroom and locks the door and starts crying. I remember Shmen telling me she's had a bout of uncontrollable peeing lately and that they don't know why.

Through the door, I tell her of all the times I peed in the wrong places. And I tell her the story of my best friend Ezra who peed in the middle of a birthday party. And I tell her the time I peed on my father and the time my father peed in his pants at age seventy-five. But she isn't comforted by my tales of incontinence.

Then this little girl comes out of the bathroom without pants, with just a shirt. "I want to be alone," she says, and she goes into Shmen and Ally's bedroom to lie down.

"Okay," I say, feeling like it was me who did the peeing.

I go in the bathroom and I take off my shirt and I lean into the tub and I wash the pee off my shirt and I wash the pee off her pants, which have already been thrown in the tub. It seemed like it was going so well and now I've got a mopey, pantsless eight-year-old on my hands. I imagine Ally coming home and me saying, "Oh, it went great. Your daughter is pantsless and in your bed. Can I have my money now?"

I nearly walk into the bedroom to comfort Maddy, but I decide to leave her alone. Sometimes, you need to give shame a little space before trying to get rid of it.

It all feels so complicated. Kids, I decide, are much different than words, which rarely urinate on you. As I wash all this urine off our clothes, as I think about how messy kids must be to raise, as I think about all the messy times with my dad and my mom, and as I think of those days with Ezra, and as I worry if Shmen is getting worse, and as I worry about how I'm going to get this novel cleaned up, and as I feel like it all is too complicated to bear, and as the smell of urine won't go away, I suddenly feel ready to have a kid with Julia.

Chapter Thirty-six
Traitors

When she picks up the phone, I say, "It's getting worse, isn't it?" I do it like they do it in the movies. I don't say hello. I don't give any introductions. I don't clear my throat. I just say what I need to say.

"He's moving out," Ally tells me. "I gave him a requirement and he couldn't live up to it."

"What do you mean? You have to look out for him." I can't imagine that this is really Ally, the person who takes care of the Fatty Lumpkins of the world. Shmen is like a thousand Fattys.

"I have to look out for Maddy," she says. "I can't live with a man who vomits in my daughter's bed while reading bedtime stories." She says it like all the boundaries in the world are so simple. And maybe they are.

Ally tells me that Shmen is moving into a nearby apartment. That she'll still do what she can to help him. They aren't even breaking up. This relieves me and makes me think that they'll work things out. Especially if I can get him drinking less. But in the same breath, she says that she's working toward having Maddy less attached to Shmen.

"Traitor," I tell her. But I say it so quietly and so empty of confidence, really I'm just trying out that word to see if it works. And it doesn't quite work.

"Yuvi," the traitoress says, "we can't force Shmen to take care of himself."

Chapter Thirty-seven
End of Business

There's a growing pile of pages on my desk.

I've been unable to spend time with Shmen. He is away from his house most of the time and even though he still calls me late at night, it's clear he doesn't want to hang out with me or Julia, which freaks Julia out even more than me. He keeps saying he needs more time but he doesn't say what he needs time for. It's like he is building a nuclear weapon in that apartment.

Julia walks into my office and looks at the pile. She probably thinks it's for her, which it sort of is, but I'm still too scared to share it. It's not ready. It's never ready.

But also, I just thought of a way to get another perspective on this book. And it doesn't even require begging a Palestinian/Clevelandian man who's smarter than me. It doesn't require anyone but me. And my manuscript. And a shitload of clothespins.

Julia kisses me on the crown of the head. And then she takes the whole pile off the table—all thirty-seven chapters. She takes the pile before I even have time to think about whether or not I'm ready to give it to her.

"Now," she says, "let me see what the hell else you've been writing about all these months." Her smile is a sneaky one.

Julia puts the pile of papers in her purse, which gives you an idea of the size of her purse, and her heels click their way to the front door.

"Wait!" I say.

The clicking stops.

"Can I do one more thing?" I say. "Can you leave the pages with me? I promise that they will be ready for you by the end of the week."

"Who do I need to crucify to finally get to see this thing?" It's her tired voice, and the tired voice is a very bad sign at 9 AM, especially after a cup of coffee.

"Give me a few more days," I say.

"Yuvi," she says, "we're on the same side."

"I know," I say, and I think about whether I know this.

My wife pulls the pile of a novel out of her purse. She holds the thing tight, wiggles it in her hand. She squats down and carefully places the pile on the floor.

"Friday," she says to the pile on the floor. "End of business Friday. Last chance." And then she clicks her way right out of the house.

Chapter Thirty-eight
Brother, Can You Spare a Palindrome?

Shmen still calls. Late. Too late.

Oh, he has important things to say. Aibohphobia is the fear of palindromes. "Spiro Agnew" and "grow a penis" are anagrams. So are "Desperation" and "A rope ends it."

Some of them are repeats, but at this hour, who's counting?

We still laugh even though he only allows for anagrams and palindromes and none of my awkward prodding about his health. Except at this hour, it's easier for me to let go of prodding and just enjoy whatever he gives me.

He also keeps talking about my novel.

"Here's your problem," he tells me. "You're getting there with the book, but you're not out of the woods yet. Your train is still rickety. There's a big matzo ball ahead."

Even though it's the telephone, I nod. He hasn't read my novel and his metaphors are dripping with *meshugas*, but I can't disagree with him either. He knows me. He knows my problems. And my problems are my novel's problems. Even so, I'm scared to ask him for more information.

"How are you feeling?" I say.

He says, "Well, it's time to go."

The phone goes click before I say goodbye.

I listen to that dial tone for a sign of things to come. And I worry that this is it. That he will be gone before we meet again.

Chapter Thirty-nine
Out to Dry

Here is how it goes: I hammer two nails on opposite walls. I tie a string between the two. Now I've got a clothesline going across my living room. I hammer two more nails. Another clothesline. And two more nails. Eventually the living room is covered with rows of strings. I open up six bags of fifty clothespins each. I bring in my thirty-nine-chapter novel and I hang each damn page up on its own clothespin. This ritual is an easy one. It only takes twenty minutes, and I don't think much of it until I stand back against the wall farthest from the pages and look at what I've got.

It's absurd to imagine this big room full of my pages crammed into a little electronic book reading device. Maybe someone else's book might fit in one of those contraptions. But my bulging, unformed mess of a book doesn't even fit in our goddamn living room.

What I've got is a thirty-nine-chapter conceit. I could have been busy trying to make millions or to save the world or to save just one soul or even to kill a dragon or even to slay the hero. What I've chosen to do is write this thing that requires 16 clotheslines, 32 nails, and 261 clothespins.

I grab all the childhood pictures of Julia I've stolen and hidden under the mattress. This includes the one with her sideways-face-smile and the one with her birthday hat that says "Everyone Loves Me" on it and the one where she has a finger up her mom's nose. I tack them up on the living room wall. And then I put the picture I stole from Yousef of his father on the wall. And then I grab those napkins I've collected, *Save Me, Julia*, which turned out to be from Shmen, and I put them up on the wall, too.

I push my desk into the living room. It involves some twisting and turning and it results in some cuts up and down my arms and hands and the taste of salt in my mouth from sucking the blood. But these are unintentional cuts, I should remind you. I feel like a vampire who has tried to become good and has stopped killing people but then comes across someone recently killed and so he sucks what's left of their blood but he has to keep reminding himself that he hasn't done anything wrong. It feels just like that.

I get a beer out of the refrigerator and then open it and then I pour the entire contents of the beer into the sink and then I hold the empty beer bottle in my hand, just for comfort. The day is getting warm and the air inside the house feels stale and I decide not to open a window. I stand up on my desk with my empty beer and look at what's in front of me.

MOUNT PISGAH

I don't remember much in the way of Hebrew teachings from Hebrew school, but what I do remember is a rabbi talking to us about Moses. How, in the end, he wasn't allowed to enter the Promised Land. Not in his lifetime. But he was able to stand on Mount Pisgah and see it. "Imagine it!" this rabbi cried out to us. "Moses could taste it between his teeth, but he couldn't swallow it!" Of course, none of us appreciated his words because we just wanted class to end. But I still remember how intense he was about this story. And from then on, I started getting dreams about Moses. No joke. I dreamed about him. Except I screwed the whole story up. In my dreams, he was standing on Stone Mountain—that granite mountain in Atlanta with the ninety-by-two-hundred-foot carving of Jefferson Davis, Robert E. Lee, and Stonewall Jackson on their horses. In the dream, Moses stood on the carving of Lee's horse (on the horse's nose actually), and he was looking out toward something that I couldn't quite see. There was something he wanted so badly and it was just out of reach. But in my dreams, it didn't seem like he was looking at a place exactly. It was more about people than place. Maybe he was just missing an old girlfriend, some gorgeous Egyptian lady with long legs that he hadn't seen in forty years. But in my dream, I never found out what he was looking for. I always woke up empty-handed.

Chapter Forty
From Up High

When my wife walks in, I'm sitting on the floor in the middle of the room and I jump to attention.

She says, "Jesus H. Tap-dancing Christ." And then she looks around the living room in silence.

"I know," I say, about her silence. And about the reference to her tap-dancing savior.

My wife walks up and down the aisles as if browsing at a secondhand store. She's in that pretty black dress with the hemline down below her knees and the hem floats off her skin as she walks. When she looks up on the wall and sees these pictures of her from thirty years ago, I hear a little gasp inside her little mouth. But she still doesn't say anything. And then she walks right up to me.

I try to play the role of the detached cashier, only mildly interested in whether she wants to buy anything. "Can I help you with anything?" I say to my dear wife.

She is almost crying. It's not that there are tears. And it's not that her eyes look moist. And it's not that she is making a crying face. But it's still there. The lips tremble if you look closely. The eyelids aren't completely opened. Her hand rests on my wrist, and she says, "You can't help me right now. Not yet."

I nod. It's all I can do. Just that one vague, three-letter gesture.

"You've written a lot," Julia says.

"Come here," I say to my wife, even though she is standing right next to me. And I grab her by her hand, which is warm from the outside world, and I bring her to the desk. We're in a particular state of mind at this point. I know this because I'm not worried about anything right now. And because Julia has not said a word about my desk being in the wrong damn room. I lift her hand and she understands this means to get up on the desk and so she gets up there. She's shaved her legs today and they are smooth except for the one little scab at the ankle.

"What do I do now?" she asks from up high on the desk.

"Look at this mess," I say, and I point all around the room for effect. "What do you see?"

Chapter Forty-one
What Do You See?

"It is a mess," Julia says from up on the desk. "No wonder your people wandered so many years in the desert."

"Thank you," I say. It's harder to hear someone else say it's a mess even though I've been using that word all these months.

Julia steps back down from the desk and then straightens out her dress. "But it's a mess with heart." When she looks at me, I understand that she has already read my novel, somehow, and that she knows exactly what happens, somehow.

"Thank you for saving my brother from the piano," she says to me.

"I couldn't let it happen to him."

"That's good," she says. "Because he's coming over for dinner and he's bringing the food."

"You convinced him to come over?" I ask. I've been having no luck with anything other than late-night calls and I'm nervous at the idea of seeing him. Feels like it's a blind date to prepare for. "Is he okay? Is it bad?"

"No," Julia says. "He actually sounds good. He said he just needed some time after moving out of Ally's place."

I'm quiet. She's quiet. We both want to believe this. But we both don't know if we should. "Good," I say, almost like a question.

"So let's see here," Julia says, browsing my manuscript again.

My wife walks among the pages. She starts at the beginning and walks along the first row while looking quickly at each page, as if speed-reading my novel. She continues along each row until she gets to the end. And then she goes back to the first row and yanks a page from the clothespin.

"Here's a problem," she says.

It's that part where I mention my mother was buried in Israel and my father was cremated—a part I tried to pull out of the damn book except whenever I pulled it out, the rest of the book kept unraveling.

"What's wrong with it?" I say.

"You haven't closed off the loose ends."

"You mean you see some ends around here?" I say, thrilled by the prospect that my novel has something worth closing. But also not excited to hear what I have to do. Probably she'll tell me that it'll take some actual work.

"First of all, you have to reconcile some things with your father," she says.

"Haven't I been doing that the whole time?"

"Sort of," she says.

Even though I'm a professional narcissist, I've learned some things about my wife at this point in the novel. Like the fact that "sort of" is a synonym for "Hell no, you stupid schmuck."

She says, "You can't just mention that a Jew gets cremated and not tell about it."

"I thought I already told about it." In this context, "I thought" is a synonym for "Stop making me feel like an even bigger schmuck than I am."

She crumples the page she is holding, drops it on the floor (clearly proving who wears the pants in this manuscript), and then walks over to the end of the novel. She goes right to

Chapter 41. "Oy," she says with the guttural sound of an old, fat Ashkenazi wise man. "You can't just leave it this way. The first step in finishing this is for you to go back to that river. See where it takes you."

I look at all the pages across this room and I consider ripping them up. I can't imagine that I have the energy to do this and I wonder why I write this stuff in the first place.

But my wife, she is unwavering. Her gentile red hair and her gentile freckles, they know me better than I know me.

Just then, I see a sadness in Julia's eyes. She says, "I can't rewrite the fact that I slept with another man. I can't rewrite the story of my mother. You can't rewrite your parents into existence. But you still have the chance to reshape your novel."

She puts a hand on her stomach. Carefully, like she doesn't want to disturb anything. I could swear that her belly has a different shape to it. And I try to think when was the last time she had a period. I realize that for all I know she hasn't had a period for the whole novel. This novel is period free. But still, something is going on in her body.

Fuck. I know I should feel a joy in all of this, but I don't. You know what I feel? Terror. Another terror on top of all the other terrors. Fuck.

"Forget it," I say, "I can't do this."

I'm not looking at her anymore. I'm looking at my pages. I grab pages from the clotheslines and I pull them out so fast that the clothespins don't even notice. So many pages on the floor that I'm slipping on them as I try to bring the whole novel down. Worse than bananas in a cartoon.

I fantasized we would be one of those couples who struggles across three years to have a baby. I wanted us to be frustrated and exhausted and required to learn all about crazy fertility issues that neither of us ever wanted to know about. I wanted that whole emotionally and financially costly mess. Because it would have bought me some more time.

"Yuvi!" the wife yells at me. "Stop it!"

She grabs me from behind and holds me so that I can't move my arms enough to grab more pages. Gentiles can be quite strong. And I stop struggling, the heat from her body pressed against me.

I take deep breaths. I know this novel can't withstand me struggling with the idea of being a parent. I haven't even told you about my nightmares where it rains foreskins. And then the idea of a little neurotic, redheaded Yuvi running around, whining even louder than me. It's too much.

"It's going to be fine," she says to me. I don't actually believe her, but I like her confidence. She must be right even if I'm sure she's wrong. If only she followed around my stream of consciousness everywhere it went.

She says, "Just take this one step at a time."

It's a tired cliché, I could never get away with a line like that in my novel, but when she says it, it feels fresh. First I go back to the river, then I finish this novel, then I learn how to change a shit-filled diaper. I don't have to do it all at once.

And then my confident wife says, "Come on. It's time to take a break. We have two hours before Shmen will be here. So let's go to bed." She grabs me by the hand, and we leave the sixteen clotheslines and all those clothespins behind.

Except for two. Because you never know when you might need a pair of makeshift nipple clamps.

ODE TO FATHER

My father didn't want to be buried like my mother was. He wanted to be burned up. He wanted to be cremated and "splashed all across the Davidson River." He told me this about three months after she died.

"What?" I said. "You can't do that. It's too late." I had my hands in fists and could feel my fingernails pressing into my palms. Jews aren't cremated—that is what I thought to say.

"It isn't the betrayal that you think it is."

"It is," I said. "Mom is buried down there waiting." This was not something I expected to say. I didn't believe in any kind of afterlife, but I still imagined my mother's rotting body, all alone down there.

"Waiting for what?" my father said. He took deep and calm breaths.

"For you," I said.

My father handed me the note. It was written on that tissue-thin paper, which my mom used for international letters, when writing to her sisters in Israel. It was a mix of my mother's English and her Hebrew.

> *I am made of adamah and you are made of miyeem and so that is where we need to go when it ends. We will meet again along the shores of the river, where the miyeem embraces the adamah.*

Her English was never so good, and her Hebrew began fading from the day I was born. But what I didn't think about was the new language she was creating between the worlds of English and Hebrew. Her story about earth and water was the kind of thing that made total sense once I read it. I wondered about all the other things she had said in my lifetime that I might have unfairly written off.

I began to cry into the tissue-thin paper. This was a kind of paper too fragile for tears. So my father pulled the note away from me. He cleaned the note with his shirt and I put myself back together.

"So you're going to do it," I said to my father, somewhere between a statement and a question.

"I think so," he said to me.

"You never wanted to be buried anyhow," I said.

"No," he said. "I guess I was just doing it for your mom. But if she would've suggested this mishugas while she was alive, I would have stopped the discussion before it started. She knew me well enough to know that the only way she could win an argument with me was to start one after she was gone."

"What about all the money you spent on that plot of land?"

My father smiled. The color of his lips was darker than I remembered. "Why?" he said. "Are you in the market for an extra burial plot?"

"No," I said. "Maybe I'll follow in your footsteps."

"Well," he said. "You better get yourself a fly rod."

#

I got the call early one morning. A heart attack. Right on the river. He died instantly, the policeman told me—a man who knew and respected my father. The man said, "One of his wooly buggers was still in his fist." He said it thinking it would make me feel better. And it did. Well, later anyway.

#

I always imagined I'd scatter his ashes alone, but in the end, it went differently. I was freshly married to Julia and had just gotten close to Shmen, and the two of them asked if they could go and support me. And I said okay.

We flew to Asheville and drove into the Pisgah National Forest, right up to the Davidson River. The forest was different than in Oregon. The pine trees were smaller, but their needles were thicker. It smelled of something sweet and sticky in the woods. There was a cold wind. The summer was nearly over, you could see it up in the tall oak trees—their leaves were green, but barely. I went up to the river and squatted beside it. The soil was spongy underneath me. I tried to read the water like my father once had. There was the noise of the water over the rocks and the ripples in the water and it was muddy in the water and the smell of the wind and the fish. But I couldn't piece it all together.

When my father squatted, when he touched his finger to the water, he saw things. "Look out there," he once said to me. "An ant has fallen off the tree." It took some time, but I saw the thing struggling on the surface of the water as the water sent him downstream. "The fish will get to him in no time," my father said.

#

I stepped into the water, not thinking that I was wearing my best pair of shoes until it was too late.

Julia stood on the bank of the river, right on the root of a tree, her hand against it like she didn't know how to stand up otherwise. This wasn't her part of the world. "I'll be right here, honey," she said, her voice a touch too quiet.

Shmen, on other the hand, fell into the water right beside me as if he had been pushed. The water at this point was still fairly shallow, only two feet deep, but deep enough so that his whole body went under.

I didn't try to save him from the fall. I was focused on the box in my hands.

He let out a yell from all the coldness in his bones. And after shaking off, he said, "I'm good. I'm cool. I'm fine. We're cool."

"I'm sorry," I said to him, as if responsible for his fall. "I should do this last thing alone."

"Yeah, brother," he said, "perhaps you should." He reached out a wet hand and put it on my shoulder. His hand was cold from the water and hot underneath the cold.

I looked back at Julia and smiled.

The box in my hands was just a small pine box no bigger than a loaf of bread. But I felt that I would drop it at any moment if I didn't direct all my attention to keeping it secure. I knew where I wanted to go.

I walked to that same bend in the river where he once apologized for hitting me with a belt. It wasn't long before I saw that rock. The one that looked like a grand piano. The one that stood above what he called Piano Pond. He once told me that the trout in Piano Pond loved one of his homemade flies. "I call it a Shmendrick bug," he said to me. "You should see it sometime. It's a beauty."

I climbed up on the rock. It was higher than I'd imagined it would be, and when I stood on it, I could see Julia and Shmen in the distance. They waved at me, but I didn't want to drop the box.

The water was muddy from all the construction upstream. A hard rain wasn't supposed to do this. That is what my dad taught me. "Nature wouldn't do it this way."

I squinted through the muddiness, watching closely for movement. I could make out two trout swimming down there.

I knew I would miss the old man who took me out to this river and showed me about ants and wooly buggers and Shmendrick bugs, but I didn't realize that I would miss the man with the belt and the angry eyes just as much. And I didn't realize that holding my father's ashes would somehow feel like a favor for my mother as well—a woman who didn't believe in cremation and wrote poetry from the grave.

There was a noise in the distance, someone calling out. Maybe Julia and Shmen, but I didn't look at them.

#

Afterward, on the flight home, I paid more attention to them. I was extra aware of how they each behaved. How Julia squeezed my hand, how she let us be so quiet together, how in her eyes were the thoughts of her own mother and father. And how Shmen handled the situation differently.

"It was the right way," Shmen said to me. He said it with a lightness in his voice. He could've been talking about a turn we had taken on the freeway.

I didn't say anything. I wasn't in the mood for social etiquette.

"The only way to die," he said, "is the way you live. At least the way you live at your best. None of this hospital horseshit."

Shmen had good intentions but I still didn't like how lightly he was talking about it. I knew he had been through some tricky times with all his surgeries and sickness but I wasn't ready to take in any life-and-death wisdom. I wanted him to talk about the hot stewardess or the number of peanuts in the complementary snack pack, not about my father dead in a river.

"And you did good," he said. "With his ashes there. He would've been proud."

I noticed on Shmen's cocktail napkin he had written something.

"What are you writing?" I asked.

"Oh, nothing," he said to me. He tried to cover it up, but I still saw what he'd written. He was always good with words, much quicker than I was.

ODE TO FATHER / EARTH FED TOO

#

Back at the river, back on that piano-shaped rock, the box was hot in my hands. I opened it carefully. When I pulled the top off, I heard the sound of air being sucked into the box. Everything my father had been was now just a few pounds of dust in a box. My eyes burned from trying so hard to look. I took the box and sprinkled the ashes into the water. One pinch at a time until all of my father was gone. The dust glistened as it fell.

It took a long time for the ashes to reach the water. And when they did, those trout came up to the surface. They inspected the ashes carefully, and then they began to nibble.

Chapter Forty-two
Peek Soul

Shmen tells us that the reason he brought us leek soup is because it's the anagram for "peek soul." He also tells us it's healthy. It's a popular recipe. It's all the rage. I'd never imagined raging leeks before. But he doesn't eat a thing. His eyes are bloodshot and his face almost seems yellow. Like the raging leek soup had already leaked into his face.

"Why aren't you eating?" Julia says, which is a secret code for saying, *Why are you drinking?*

"Oh," Shmen says. He waves his hand in the air, does some odd spiraling gesture. "I ate back at the office."

This line is so broken that Julia doesn't even begin to dissect it. She closes her eyes and breathes. I wish I could down a few drinks to tolerate the meal. Instead of drinking alcohol, I stand up, kiss my wife on the head. And then I go to the bathroom.

I don't even crave cutting myself, I just want to sit on the toilet and wait for all of this to pass. But I know it won't. I'll have to do something to make it better. So I flush the toilet to make it seem like something has happened here.

When I come back out, Julia's full bowl of soup is sitting in the kitchen sink and she is back at her seat.

"How many times have we talked about this?" she says to Shmen. She is gripping her spoon and shaking it at her

brother. It's the kind of thing they probably tell you not to do
when counseling someone with a problem.

"You've said it quite a lot," he says as if he isn't being
threatened by a spoon. "But life," he says, "is a lot like a horse
with a big uncontrollable dick."

To laugh was not the right thing to do. I know I shouldn't
have laughed.

Julia puts her hand on her belly at this moment. And then
she says, "I'm sorry." And she walks right out of the kitchen.

#

Shmen and I sit there in the kitchen for a few minutes. I spend
the time trying to come up with an angle. Some approach to the
situation. Some graceful entry. I think of all the techniques Julia
has told me about when she talks to her patients. But I come up
with nothing. I use the approach of having no approach.

"So is it as bad as it looks?" I ask him.

"Yeah," he says. He nods, but his head doesn't move as
much as a proper nod requires. "Probably worse than it looks.
Did you know that I'm blind in one eye? Can you tell that I
can barely turn my body? Can you see that it is hard to breathe
because my ribs won't expand?"

"Holy fuck," I say.

"It's okay," he says. "The alcohol makes it hurt less."

"What about a doctor? There must be a treatment."

"I'm done with those guys," he tells me. "I'm off the grid
and going further."

I turn this over a few times. I don't get the grid metaphor
but what I get is that my brother-in-law is done with trying to
find remedies for his esoteric diseases.

And then something happens that I don't expect. He asks
me a question. He lets me in further. "Brother," he says, "will
you skidoo me a favor?"

"Yes," I say, almost before he finishes asking.

"I don't want to go with a fused spine or pulmonary fibrosis or lung disease or by drinking myself stupid. I want to go with a wooly bugger in my fist."

Chapter Forty-three
Save Me, Julia

It's late. Julia and I are lying in bed. We've spent an hour talking about Shmen. She's been crying. "I should be better at this," she says. "I see this kind of thing every day. But it's like I've learned nothing that helps with my own brother."

"It's always different with family," I say. And I know it's a dumb thing to say, but it's a true dumb thing.

I put my hand on Julia's belly. She flinches when I touch her. Usually, she's not into me touching her like that. But after the initial jump, she lets my hand rest there.

"Why didn't you tell me?" I say.

She doesn't answer for long enough that I wonder if she heard me. And then: "It's too soon," she says. "Seven weeks in. Anything can happen from here." She breathes a few times and her belly goes up and down. "And I was scared to tell you. I don't know if you're ready. I don't know if *we're* ready."

"I don't know either," I say. "But I think it's a bad idea to wait until a man like me is ready."

I wouldn't have noticed the laugh without my hand on her diaphragm.

"In any case," I say, "I'm glad to not be ready with you."

"Thank you," she says.

I sit up and look down at my wife.

"What is it?" she says.

"Do you buy into this crazy *shtuyot* that we should look out for the people we love? Even if it's heartbreaking for us to do what we think is right?" I make it sound like a trick question, which it obviously is. It's actually such a dumb trick question that it might even be tricky.

I reach down to her belly. I rub her belly around in a circle like I'm looking for answers in there.

"Yes," my wife says. "I buy it."

She's getting concerned. I can tell. Even in the dark I see her eyebrows go all wiggly.

I kiss my wife on the lips. It's a good, arrogant, passionate kiss. I taste the leek soup and the toothpaste and some mysterious strawberry flavor.

And then I get up. I leave that warm, maybe-with-a-baby body of hers.

"I'll be right back," I say.

"Where you going?"

"To close off some loose ends," I say, and walk out of the room like I know what I'm doing. I step into the living room and look at the mess of papers on the clotheslines and on the floor. But I don't scrutinize the pages. I grab a napkin and a pen from a drawer in my desk and stick them in my pocket. I also grab the pack of cigarettes and the lighter, both stashed in the back of another drawer.

I light a cigarette and then walk outside, careful to open and close the door quietly.

Chapter Forty-four
A Banished Typo

"Thanks for sticking around," I say to Shmen. He is waiting on the sidewalk by our house.

"Took you long enough," he says. "I worried that you were waiting for the messiah to arrive."

I point the pack of cigarettes in his direction and he shakes his head.

"No thanks," he says. "Those things will kill you."

"I know."

"You'll be a fabulous father," he says. He gives me a thumbs-up and a wink. It's an odd gesture that would look insincere coming from anyone else, and maybe it's because of the odd state he is in, but it's so sweet that it momentarily alleviates my terror of parenting.

"How did you know?"

"I know things," he says. He looks past me, as if he expected me to bring a group of people. "So how does this go exactly?"

I sit down on the curb, spit out the disgusting cigarette, and put my face in my hands. "This is wrong," I say.

"It's the right way." Shmen pats me on the head. "You know it."

I stand up and grab my brother-in-law. I hug him. He is thicker and more muscular than I expected. I don't think I've ever felt closer to anyone. He grabs me so tightly that it makes it hard to breathe.

When he pulls out of the hug, he says, "Do you have all the details worked out for Maddy and Ally?"

"Yes," I say, giving myself a moment of peace while thinking about Maddy. "They'll be millionaires from this."

"Good," he says. "So what did you bring with you? A gun? A knife? An axe? A rectal probe? A bomb?"

I reach into my pockets and grab the napkin and the pen and hand them to him. "Make it good," I say.

My brother-in-law smiles with even his ears rising from the way it pleases him. I'll never forget that look. "Brilliant," he says.

He sits on the curb and writes something on the napkin and hands it back to me. It says: a banished typo.

"What the hell does this mean?"

"You'll figure it out," he says. And he kisses me on the lips. His lips are warm and taste like vodka and tangerines.

The ground starts to shake. A rumbling builds in the distance.

Shmen runs out into the street. He runs so easily, his joints as limber as ever, all of his diseases momentarily gone. He stands in the middle of the street. He shakes both his hands quickly as he prepares himself. I hear him repeating the phrase "A banished typo" over and over again.

He gives me one last look.

Winks, even.

I say, "Stop!" But it's only a whisper. And of course my one powerless little word can't save him.

A dozen pianos—Steinway grands, this time—race down the street. Shmen looks them straight on, without a hint of fear. The brass wheels of the pianos squeal against the asphalt as they get close to him, like they are trying to stop. But it's too late.

And then a dozen 750-pound pianos hit my brother, one after another, each exploding into its 12,000 pieces as it hits him. He stands there, solid, like a stone wall. And the piano pieces, the thick mahogany legs, the flailing steel strings, the felt-covered hammers, the brass pedals, the enormous lids, the drizzle of black and white keys, the whole musical disaster flies up in the air and hangs up there with a kind of silence, until all the pieces crash to the ground with a beautiful, horrible noise. When the last of the pieces falls to the earth, my brother falls too. He falls like all the bones inside of him have been sucked out.

Piles of piano pieces all around. Not a drop of blood coming from his body. He never was a bleeder.

#

I sit next to my brother amidst the mess of pianos in the middle of the street, holding his hand, which has grown cold by the time the ambulance arrives.

I honestly don't know how any of us will make it through a world without Shmen. He was the strongest one.

But also, all my terrors seem a bit pointless now. They're still there. But they just don't have the same power. I have to take care of more serious matters. For Maddy, and Ally, and for Julia, and that maybe kid that I'm maybe going to have.

I let go of Shmen's hand and stand up to greet the man who has just jumped from the ambulance. I lick my lips and taste the vodka tangerine flavor of Shmen's kiss.

The emergency men don't ask me much. They know what's happened here. It's the same old story. So they focus on Shmen and his body. And I watch them carefully: even after they know it's hopeless, they do everything in their power to save him.

#

When I finally climb into bed, it's almost morning, and Julia is asleep, curled up in the opposite direction. I don't bother taking off my clothes. I pull the napkin message out of my pocket and look at it for a few more seconds. I miss Shmen terribly but I also know it's too soon to feel the real ache. The earth is still shaking. I place the napkin on the nightstand and then curl up around my wife. I put my arm around her.

And that's when I realize that she is crying so hard that the entire bed is bouncing from her sobs. I squeeze her tight and she keeps crying and we grieve together in the dark.

#

When I wake up the next morning, the sun is shockingly bright and my wife is no longer in the bed. I get this sudden relief that maybe it was all a dream.

But then I see that fucking napkin on the nightstand.

The napkin is marked up, covered in my wife's notes. She has scribbled all over the thing and it takes me a while to realize that she has solved Shmendrick's anagram.

A BANISHED TYPO — DEATH BY PIANOS

I stand up quickly. There's so much that needs to be done. Good thing I kept my pants on.

Acknowledgements.

This book was born at the Pinewood Table, where Stevan Allred and Joanna Rose lead one hell of a workshop. I learned so much from you two.

Cheryl Strayed. You helped me get this book out into the world. Thank you for your relentless support of me and my writing.

To my literary manager, Rayhané Sanders, for being a real champion of this book and my writing. And to my editor, Guy Intoci, for his faith in this book and for making it better.

Liz Prato, thank you for too many things, including our emergency check-ins. Jackie Shannon Hollis, our gossipy literary dinners. Laura Stanfill, Sarah Cypher, Shanna Germain in that Year of the Novel. Scott Sparling, your fabulous insane writing. Kate Gray, I knew you were incredible from that first workshop. Suzy Vitello, for great conversations and great advice and grappa. Christi Krug, your grace. Tammy Stoner, those great cocktails and conversations. Ellen Urbani, for truly bad ass feedback. To Tom Spanbauer, who has influenced many who have influenced me. Steve Taylor, I ache for our post-workshop wine sessions.

To my Antioch mentors: Leonard Chang, your pointed feedback was viciously valuable, and Alistair McCartney, you taught me a new way to see the particulars. Rob Roberge, who doesn't realize I'm still angry I didn't score mentorship time with him. Steve Heller, for allowing my ass into the MFA program.

Kate Maruyama, for all your kindness and damn fine insights. Jae Gordon, Stephanie Westphal, your support and love and more. Telaina Eriksen, for those fireside chats (I'm still resentful for the one that got interrupted). Stephanie Glazier, your great fabulosity and brilliant glow. Kristen Forbes, I miss our 'writing' sessions. To the fucking Sages.

Mom, Dad, hope my love shows even if I twisted many stories. Dan, I owe you for all the mileage your intestines gave me, and much more.

Sheri Blue. For a million things, on paper and especially not on paper. Dashiell, to you too. And of course to Savi, who does not yet realize how bald and worried his father really is.